Cross Country Christmas

A Woodfalls Girls Novella

BY

TIFFANY KING

www.authortiffanyjking.blogspot.com

Cross Country Christmas

Cover by Okay Creations
Cover Photo by Abby Blom
Edited by Hollie Westring

All rights reserved. Published by A.T. Publishing LLC
Copyright © 2013 by Tiffany King

License Notes

This ebook is licensed for your personal enjoyment only. This ebook may not be re-sold or given away to other people. If you would like to share this book with another person, please purchase an additional copy for each recipient. If you're reading this book and did not purchase it, or it was not purchased for your use only, then please purchase your own copy. Thank you for respecting the hard work of this author.

All rights reserved. Except as permitted under the U.S. Copyright Act of 1976, no part of this publication may be reproduced, distributed, or transmitted in any form or by any means, or stored in a database or retrieval system, without the prior written permission of the publisher.

The characters and events portrayed in this book are fictitious. Any similarity to real persons, living or dead, is coincidental and not intended by the author.

ACKNOWLEDGMENTS

Thank you to my readers and friends who support me each and every day.

And to my family who inspire me.

Without you none of this is possible.

Dreams Do Come True…Dream Big <3

CHAPTER 1

The large roaring engines of the surrounding planes vibrated the Jetway beneath my feet. I wasn't the biggest fan of flying anyway, and the airlines didn't make it any easier. They funnel you down a narrow tunnel, through a narrow opening, down a narrow aisle, and then make you sit in a narrow seat where you have an elbow face-off with a stranger for a narrow armrest. I'm a fairly petite person and even I feel like a tightly wrapped sushi roll. My rolling suitcase that was stuffed with everything I would need for two weeks in Woodfalls bounced off the heels of my feet every time the woman in front of me stopped to pacify her screaming toddler. Yet another part of flying that had me regretting I didn't have a stiff drink at the airport Chili's before boarding. Don't get me wrong, I liked kids. Heck, I plan to have my own one day when I finally find Mr. Right. I say "one day" because so far, I haven't had the best luck in the dating arena, and now I was returning to Woodfalls for the holidays where the pickings were pretty slim. How I had allowed my mom and my cousin Tressa to talk me into returning home for Christmas was beyond me. I had sworn after the guilt-fest that ensued last year that I would take a year off from holidays in Woodfalls. Of course, my mom had pried her way through my defenses like she always did. She had a way of making it nearly impossible to say no. Next year, I would stick to my guns. Yeah, I'm as sure of that as I am that I'll win the lottery. It's not like I didn't love Woodfalls, or even my family for that matter. I'm just tired of returning as a single gal every year. Since I was a little girl, I've pictured myself marrying the perfect guy and raising our three kids— one girl and two boys—in Woodfalls. Growing up, my parents' marriage had been a measuring stick for me, and I knew that was the kind of relationship I wanted. I always assumed when I returned home from college it would be to settle down and start a family. At the rate I was going, I'd be returning to Woodfalls as a wrinkly old cat lady.

As I continued to inch my way down the aisle of the plane, waiting for slow-moving passengers to stuff their oversized bags into the overhead compartments, I sighed with resigned acceptance that eventually I would reach my seat at the back of the plane. That's what I got for waiting until the last minute to book my flight. I could have driven, but that would only give my mom and aunt an excuse to try talking me into staying in Woodfalls longer. That was one of the downfalls of being a food blogger. My job could be done from anywhere, and my mom reminded me of that every chance she got.

I finally spotted my row at the back of the plane. Go figure. The harried mom and screaming toddler ended up being in the row directly in front of mine. That seemed to be my relationship with karma. At least it was only an hour and a half flight. I guess I could survive for that long.

Lifting my suitcase, I staggered slightly under its weight. *Why couldn't I learn to pack lighter?* I silently chastised myself.

"Here, let me," a warm masculine voice said as he reached up over me to stow my suitcase effortlessly into the overhead compartment.

Hmmm, strong is good. I thought, taking in the exposed forearms that were bracketing me on both sides. Maybe flying home wasn't the worse idea after all. Now, would he be as cute as he sounded?

"Why, thank you," I drawled, twisting around so I could introduce myself to my rescuer. My throat closed in on me the moment our eyes met, making the end of my statement come out as more of a gasp. Cute wasn't the issue. In fact, he was downright handsome. The problem was the familiarity of the face staring back at me. Of all the craptastic luck.

"Hello, Jams," he drawled back, observing my dismay with an amused expression.

"It's Jamie," I replied through gritted teeth, claiming my seat, but not before I smacked my head on the overhang above me. "Mother of all suck," I yelped, grabbing my head.

"Whoa, careful there," he chuckled loudly. "Remember, there are children nearby," he laughed as I let out a string of swear words that had the mother in the next row glaring at me between the seats.

Damn, Grant. He seemed to have a knack for seeing me at my worst. I rubbed my throbbing forehead, wondering how things could get any more awkward. This is why I left Woodfalls in the first place. Finding a man who didn't know everything about me was a must. The small population of Woodfalls offered limited choices for a future husband, and because everyone in town knew each other, it didn't leave much to the imagination. Take Grant Johnson sitting next to me. He'd seen my panties way before it was acceptable. I was eight years old when an unfortunate upside-down hanging attempt on the monkey bars left my skirt over my head, revealing my day-of-the-week panties. For months after that Grant would ask me every day what day of the week it was. Go figure that would happen around him. It was devastating at the time, considering he was my very first crush. Not that I would have ever admitted that to him. The little jerk was relentless and even though he eventually forgot about the panties, he found many other things to tease me about. Like how I may have gotten a little overzealous while plucking my eyebrows when I was twelve. To say they were sparse would have been a pretty generous description. Only a couple of hairs were left over each of my eyes. That provided Grant with ammunition for weeks. I went home that first day in tears, vowing to never talk to him again. I even crossed out his name along with all the little hearts I had drawn in my diary. From that day forward, I pretended he no longer existed. At least my lack of response took the fun out of any future teasing and Grant moved on to messing with Amanda Halt. For years after that, I pretty much stayed off his radar, which I thought I was okay with until Grant and Amanda started dating freshman year. Then it felt like a kick in the gut. Sure, it was years later, but technically, I was the reason he noticed her in the first place. I felt like I should have had dibs or something. Realizing the insanity of my reasoning, I turned my sights to the other guys in town, but none of them sparked my interest like Grant had. It was finally during senior year, after the typical round robin method of teenage dating, I came to the conclusion that the guys in Woodfalls just didn't have what I was looking for. I knew all of them too well. It was like dating a relative or something. So, I left Woodfalls the first opportunity I got and vowed not to return until I had found the perfect guy for me.

"How's the head, Jams?" Grant asked, sliding into the seat next to me.

"It's fine," I lied. My head was throbbing like a tequila hangover. "What are you doing on this plane?" I asked ungraciously as he stretched out his long legs in the cramped space that airlines claimed was ample legroom.

"Why, is this your plane?" he asked, looking amused.

"Ha-ha, smart-ass. I meant, why aren't you in Woodfalls?"

"Wait, this isn't Woodfalls?" he teased.

"Hilarious. Are you ever serious?"

"Not if I can help it. I was out of town for business. Man, how crazy is it that we end up on the same flight?" he threw back at me.

"Yeah, crazy. Of all the planes in all the world," I said, tapping my foot nervously as the engines began to roar louder. The plane slowly backed away from our gate. This was by far the worst part of flying for me. Taxiing down the runway followed by the instant acceleration and the ascent into the air always makes my stomach drop to my ankles. I wanted to run down the aisle and flail at the door until they let me out, but instead I dug my nails into my thighs. Once we reached our cruising altitude, I would be fine. Continuing the death grip on my legs, I clamped my eyes closed and silently sang my favorite Mumford & Sons song in my head. It was a ritual that helped me cope with my nerves. Usually, by the time I hit the last line we were well into the sky.

"You okay, Jams?" I faintly heard Grant ask. I was too busy singing in my head to give him any real acknowledgment. I merely nodded without opening my eyes and continued with my internal concert. I could feel my body reacting to the high revving engines. The worst part was upon us. We were putting our fate in the hands of someone we had never met. The plane picked up speed, pushing me back into my seat and I felt the tires lift off the tarmac.

Grant reached for my hand, but I didn't have the willpower at the moment to jerk away. I just wanted us to get in the air. The song in my head was finishing its last chorus, and at any moment I could breathe again. Then maybe I would remove Grant's hand, which was resting on top of mine.

The thought had no sooner filtered through my head when a sudden earth-shattering bump made our plane lurch forward. The seatbelt bit into my stomach as my body was thrown forward like I was a rag doll. Some of the overhead compartments flew open, sending bags shooting out. A poor old man in the aisle seat two rows up held his nose with blood dripping from behind his fingers after a small rolling suitcase dropped from the compartment across from him. Grant's hand dug into mine as he gripped the arm of the seat. Panic-filled screams echoed through the plane as we took a sudden nosedive toward the runway we had just left. The toddler in front of me shrieked. I wanted to join him, but I couldn't muster the breath from my lungs. The nose of the plane slammed hard against the tarmac and the deafening sound of metal grinding against asphalt overtook the screaming passengers. All my senses rose to a fever pitch. We were going to die. It was my worst fear. I was stuck in this metal death trap, about to meet death and I was still single. The plane continued to race down the runway as more luggage fell from the overhead compartments. Grant twisted his body to protect me from the falling debris. Eventually, the plane's momentum stalled and we finally shuttered to a stop. Gasps of pain by those who had been hit by flying luggage could be heard throughout the aircraft, but the sighs of relief that we were not going to die was much louder.

Chapter 2

A moment of silence settled over the plane as we ground to a stop. Even the crying baby in front of me seemed to take a breath. The fleeting moment quickly erupted to mayhem as passengers began standing. One of the two flight attendants tried to calm everyone, asking if anyone was seriously hurt or in need of medical attention.

"Are you okay?" Grant asked, cupping my face in his hands so I would have to focus on his words. It was only at that moment that I realized I was shaking from head to toe. "We're okay," he said, removing an article of clothing that didn't belong to me from my lap. He tossed it in the aisle that was now slanting toward the front of the plane.

I didn't answer as I spotted the wound on his forehead. I watched with morbid fascination as the blood trickled down his face in a slow stream. It began to pool on his shoulder, changing the light blue material of his shirt to more of a plum color. The crimson stain continued to grow as more blood collected there.

"Jams, are you okay?" Grant repeated with concern clouding his voice. I finally pulled my eyes from his shoulder. I was surprised he seemed so concerned about me. He hardly looked in my direction the entire time we were in high school, and now suddenly he was looking at me like I was the most important person in the world to him.

I wanted to nod my head, but at the moment, I was anything but okay. My head refused to move. I couldn't focus and everything around me looked like a kaleidoscope. I was only seeing fragments of what was really in front of me. I knew I should move. I wanted off this death trap, but I couldn't seem to will my body to make it happen. Things became hazy after that. Grant stopped asking if I was okay, and instead took matters into his own hands. I don't remember much about getting off the plane. One minute, I was buckled in my seat, and the next I was in some holding area in the airport with all the other passengers from the flight. Medical personnel were working and taking stock of various injuries from the accident. For the most part, everyone was okay except for a flight attendant who had suffered a broken leg and a concussion from a food cart that had gotten away.

"Miss, do you need to go to the hospital?" a kind paramedic asked, breaking through the haze in my mind. He shined a light in my eyes to check my pupils. "Hey, can you hear me? Are you hurt?"

It took me a moment to find my voice. "No, I'm fine," I answered. It came out as more of a croak. I cleared my throat and tried again as he wrapped my bicep to check my blood pressure.

"Just relax while I check you over a little," he said.

"I'm okay," I repeated, looking up at Grant, who was still hovering over me. His head now sported a bandage where they had treated his wound. I was surprised they weren't taking him in for stitches. "What about you?" I asked him, looking at the stark white bandage.

"It was more superficial. No stitches necessary," he answered, looking relieved that I was no longer comatose. "Are you sure you don't need to go to the hospital?" he asked, looking to the paramedic for confirmation. "Do you think she's in shock?" Grant asked, like I wasn't there.

"Probably a little, but her vitals are okay. Did she pass out?"

"No, but she's been pretty foggy since the crash," Grant answered.

"Well, her skin is not clammy and her breathing seems normal, but we can bring her in if you're concerned."

"I'm fine," I answered, done with them acting like I was a child.

The paramedic looked at Grant like my opinion didn't matter. I was tempted to kick him since he was still kneeling in front of me, but I figured that wouldn't help my case. Grant nodded hesitantly, even though he had no right to be making judgment calls on anything to do with my health or my body. I refrained from pointing that out since my brain was finally beginning to sort through what had happened.

First, I thought I better call my mom to let her know. The last thing I needed was for the accident to make national news and for her to find out before I had a chance to call her. I reached for my purse to grab my phone, only to realize my purse was still stowed under the seat on the plane. "Damn," I said. Why didn't I grab it before we left the plane? My oversized purse had everything important in it—my phone, my wallet and my iPad. The thought of functioning without my stuff even for a moment filled me with a whole new sense of panic.

I rose to my feet, intending to find it. I swayed slightly from the sudden movement.

"Whoa, where you going?" Grant asked, reaching a hand out to steady me.

"My purse. I need it," I answered, not caring that I sounded like some junkie looking for her next fix. I wanted my purse, like NOW.

"You'll have to wait. They said they'll be moving all the bags and luggage into a holding area as soon as the plane is safe enough," Grant said, plopping down on the seat I had just vacated. He stretched out his legs and yawned loudly like he had nothing better to do than wait.

Now would have been a good time to have my purse since I had the urge to hit him upside the head with it. "Did they say how long it's going to be?" I asked, steadying myself with the arm of the chair.

"Like a couple of hours, probably. What's your deal? Do you need to hit the john?" he asked as I did my "I'm dying without my phone" dance.

"Still not funny. I happen to need my purse more than the average person," I stated, looking around for anyone who could help me. The airport staff were scattered about, but seemed to have more important duties than to retrieve lost purses at the moment.

    Grant's indifference swiftly changed to concern as he stood up to help me search. "I didn't realize you needed it that bad. Is it for health reasons or something? I should have grabbed it before we left the airplane," he said, spotting a flight attendant across the room. "Let me see if we can get you what you need," he threw over his shoulder as I watched him stride purposefully for help.

    Crap, he thought I needed medicine or something from my bag. Embarrassment flooded me. I should have called him back, but my desire to have my phone outweighed my remorsefulness. Besides, it wasn't my fault he had misunderstood me. I never said I had medicine in my purse. All I had said was I needed it more than the average person, which was technically true. My entire business was run by the electronic devices in my bag.

    I was still rooted to the same spot when Grant returned, looking concerned. "They're going to see about getting you your bag. Are you feeling okay? Maybe you should go to the hospital. I'm sure they will have the medication you need on hand."

I shifted my weight to my other foot, feeling like a complete ass. I couldn't believe how concerned he was. "It's not medication I need from my bag," I admitted.

"It's not?" he asked. His eyebrows came together with confusion.

"No, I need my iPad and my phone."

"Are you serious? I thought you were diabetic or something," he said through gritted teeth.

"I need to call my mom, but I also make a living on those devices, so you can wipe that look off your face," I said in a huff.

We both watched the flight attendant talking to an airport official as she pointed in my direction.

"Great, what did you tell her?" I asked under my breath.

"What do you think I told them? I thought you *needed* your bag."

"Well, I do," I said defensively, though the guilt was now gnawing at me.

He looked at me incredulously for a minute. "For your phone."

"Well, you should have asked before charging off like some knight in shining armor."

He muttered something under his breath that I didn't quite catch, but I ignored him. I felt guilty over the mix-up, but a part of me still just wanted my bag. Time slowly trickled by and after a half an hour passed, it became clear finding my purse wasn't a priority. I watched with envy as Grant extracted his phone from his pocket and proceeded to make a call. I didn't have to attempt to eavesdrop since he didn't seem to care that everyone in the vicinity could hear him. The conversation sounded one-sided as Grant only interrupted occasionally to reassure the person on the other line that he was okay. I felt an odd stirring in the pit of my stomach. I didn't want to admit I was jealous that he obviously had a special someone who cared for him and I had no one. I was proud of the success I had reached with my business, but it didn't change the fact that when I left Woodfalls four years ago, I thought it was only a matter of time until I found Mr. Right. I wanted a relationship like my parents had, one that stood the test of time and was an equal amount of give and take. Now, five years later, I had dated enough guys to realize that Mr. Right was tougher to find than I thought.

My spirits perked up when I heard him address the person on the other line. He was talking to his mother. *Thank goodness. Wait, that was harsh,* I thought. It wasn't like his love life was any of my business. It was all but a given in high school that he would marry Amanda when we graduated, which was one of the reasons I had hightailed it out of Woodfalls. Even now, I made a point anytime I talked to my cousin Tressa to never ask about it. Only one person in Woodfalls knew about my past crush on Grant, and I knew that person would take that secret to the grave.

He gave his mom one more reassurance before hanging up. "My mom," he acknowledged after hanging up his phone, not that I needed the clarification. I nodded, though my eyes were focused on his phone. He grinned mischievously, wagging his phone in front of me. "Did you want to use my phone?" he asked. I reached out to snatch it, but he pulled it just out of reach. "Say please," he teased.

"Please," I said through a fake smile. This was the Grant I remembered, always the tease. I made another grab for the phone.

"And you're sorry you deceived me before," he added, pulling the phone away again.

I glared at him before turning away. He could shove his damn phone for all I cared. This was why he had infuriated me so much in school.

"Here, I was kidding," he said, holding the phone in front of my face.

I made no move to grab it. I knew him too well. I knew once I tried, he would move it again. Sucker me couldn't help myself. He moved it at the last second—of course.

"Say it," he taunted.

"God, are you ever going to grow up?" I fumed, glaring out the large window.

"Do you mean am I ever going to become uptight like some people?" he asked, looking at me pointedly. "I sure hope not," he added, shuddering dramatically. "Don't you get sick of always taking life so seriously?"

"We're adults, Grant. It's what adults do."

"It's what adults do," he mocked in a deep voice. "Oh my god. Obviously you're not hearing yourself. You're twenty-three, not forty-three. I bet you were a barrel of laughs in college," he laughed.

"You got me. I wasn't going to a keg party every night to hone my beer bong skills, so what? Excuse me for deciding it was better to get the education I was paying for," I snapped. Of course, I was lying through my teeth, but he didn't need to know that. Better for him to think I was a stick in the mud than to know how many parties I had attended, hoping to meet that one special person. After two years of the same crap, I was sick of the whole party scene and the college experience in general. I transferred to culinary school and focused on my career while I formulated plan B. Everything sort of clicked after that, at least professionally. Not long into my schooling, I came up with the idea to start a blog showcasing some of my favorite recipes. I named the blog Cooking for Love. After all, the old saying claims the way to a man's heart is through his stomach. I post meal prep videos twice a week, but the rest of the time I leave helpful hints on making yummy treats for your loved one. I also encourage followers to ask me questions and email their ideas. Once a month, I pick one of the ideas and prepare it on my site. The author of the winning recipe receives credit for the meal, a bottle of wine and chocolate-covered strawberries. My giveaways became an instant hit and each month the number of entries doubled from the previous month. Two and half years later, I've managed to build my blog into a successful business, but ironically, I haven't been able to cook my way into a man's heart.

"Never underestimate the mad skills it takes to become a champion beer-bonger," Grant said, standing up. He walked away dialing his phone and my stomach twisted into knots. It didn't take an Einstein to figure out who he was calling. Looking away, I studied the other passengers who sat with nothing more to do than wait like I was. I wondered how the crash would affect their lives. I shuddered to think if we would be sitting here if our plane had reached thirty thousand feet before whatever the malfunction was happened. I'm sure many of the other passengers were thinking the same thing.

"Here," Grant said, appearing at my side quicker than I expected. He dropped his phone on my lap before heading toward the bathroom. Maybe Amanda didn't answer his call. I dialed my parents' number and my mom answered immediately, like she had been waiting for the phone to ring. She sounded relieved when she heard my voice, but after she was certain I was okay, she chastised me for waiting so long to call her. It took me awhile to get her to pipe down long enough to let me explain what happened. My palms began to sweat as I recalled the fear of death I felt when the plane nosedived.

"What are you going to do now?" her voice interrupted my wayward thoughts.

"I'm not sure. Definitely not flying," I answered since the mere thought of stepping into another plane had me teetering on the edge of hysteria.

"But I want you home for Christmas," my mom all but wailed through the phone. "Especially after what happened today. I need my baby here."

"I know, Mom. I'm still coming. I think I'll rent a car. I can make the trip in one day if I don't stop."

"Dear, I'm not crazy about you driving all by yourself."

"Mom, I drive by myself all the time," I reminded her as Grant sank down in the seat next to mine.

"I understand that, honey, but driving halfway across the country isn't safe for any woman, especially after what you've been through."

"It's not halfway across the country," I pointed out. I refrained from reminding her that she's the one who wanted me to drive. When she started her worry mode, there was no reasoning with her. I listened with half an ear as she continued to bemoan my predicament. Only when she suggested that she could fly here to make the drive with me, did I intervene. I would have laughed at her suggestion, but I knew she was dead serious. A mixture of amusement and dismay swirled through me. Don't get me wrong. I loved my parents dearly, but the idea of my *mommy* flying in to rescue me didn't sit right. "Mom, don't be ridiculous. I don't need you to fly here and hold my hand. The drive isn't that long," I explained. I shushed Grant, who was chuckling beside me. He wiggled his fingers in my face to get on my nerves until I elbowed him in the gut. You'd think he would have gotten the hint, but it only egged him on further. I swatted his hand away as I continued to try to convince my mom that I was indeed capable of driving myself to Woodfalls. I was in the middle of reminding her of all the traveling I had done the last few years when Grant plucked the phone from my hand.

"Don't you even do it," I threatened. I was shocked he had the nerve to snatch the phone from me.

He held up a hand to quiet my complaints, and for the first time in my life, I contemplated murder. I tried to retrieve the phone before he could speak, but once he stood up, he was too tall. All I managed to do was draw attention to us as I practically crawled up his body in an attempt to get the phone.

"Mrs. Lawton, this is Grant Johnson," he said into the phone. I could hear my mom's happy squeal from my seat. I rolled my eyes. For whatever reason, all the adults in Woodfalls had always liked Grant. Even when I used to complain about his endless teasing, my mom had always defended him, telling me that was his way of showing he liked me. She was wrong. I was nothing but a source of entertainment for him. "We were both on the flight," he said into the phone. "I know, small world, right? Me and Jams together," he added. I'm sure he didn't mean his words to sound the way they did, but it still didn't stop my pulse from racing slightly. Grant's next words made my blood pressure rise. I had to have heard him wrong because there was no way in hell he could have been serious. Otherwise, I really was going to have to kill him now.

Chapter 3

"Are you insane?" I hissed as he ended the phone call with my mom.

"What?" he asked, feigning surprise.

"There's no way I'm driving eight hundred plus miles with you."

"Nine-nineteen," he corrected, stowing the phone back in his pocket.

"What?" I asked, momentarily distracted as I watched the phone disappear from sight.

"It's nine hundred and nineteen miles to be exact. I Googled it," he said, patting his pocket.

"It doesn't matter if it's nine miles. I'm not driving anywhere with you," I stated. There was no way I could spend that much time with him. Eventually, we would move past the superficial talking we had been doing. I didn't want to delve into what he had been up to in my absence from Woodfalls. More specifically, I didn't want to hear about his perfect little life with Amanda. I would have continued my objection, but a team of airport personnel entered the holding area.

"Why not?" he asked as we joined the semicircle of passengers that had formed around the airport employees.

"Um, could it be because you made my preteen years hell?" I said, grasping for any excuse I could come up with. He started to argue, but I shushed him so I could hear what the airport staff had to say. Most of it didn't pertain to me since I had no interest in catching a new flight. All I cared about was getting my luggage and getting out of this airport. The spokesperson for the airline talked in a loud voice that carried through the large room. She first apologized for the trauma we had all suffered. She claimed they were doing everything in their power to get all of us to our destinations, yada yada yada. Once she had covered new flights and how the airline would compensate us with free flight vouchers, she moved to an explanation about the accommodations they had secured for those of us who would not be catching a flight that night. Finally, she got to something I actually cared about, collecting our belongings. They had a shuttle waiting to take us to the hangar where they had placed all our bags.

Without giving any thought to Grant, I was the first to step in line for the shuttle. I planned on finding my bags and getting the heck out of Dodge. Alone.

"Not so fast, Jams," Grant said, joining me.

"I think the end of the line is back there," I said, pointing over my shoulder.

"You're not leaving the airport without me."

"First of all, this isn't the line to leave the airport. Second, you're the only one who thinks we're leaving together," I pointed out, tapping my fingers impatiently against my leg as I waited for them to show us to our shuttle.

"Not true. I promised your mom I wouldn't let you drive home by yourself," he said, holding up a hand when I tried to argue. "And I never break a promise," he continued. He looked serious. It was the first time I could recall seeing him without a trace of teasing.

"Look, Grant. I appreciate the offer. Really, I do, but I'm a big girl. I've been on my own long enough now. Driving through a couple of states by myself is no biggie. Trust me. You know how protective my mom has always been."

"All that being said, it's still not a bad idea for us to drive together. We are going to the same place. Just think, if we ride together, we can share the driving duties and get there even faster," he reasoned as an employee led us out to the airport shuttle.

"Yeah, but you're forgetting something important," I said, climbing onto the large bus.

"What is that?" he asked, sitting down on the bench seat next to me.

I looked at him incredulously. Was he being obtuse on purpose, or was he really that dense? "We don't like each other," I answered, gripping the metal handrail to steady myself as the shuttle came to an abrupt halt.

"Who said I didn't like you, Jams?" he asked, reaching a hand down to help me get to my feet. A couple things happened simultaneously at that moment. One, I had never seen him look so sincere, and two, the feeling of my hand being wrapped inside his large and very masculine hand made my stomach twirl. Our eyes met for a brief instant before I pulled my hand away and scrambled out of the seat and down the aisle. In my haste to leave the shuttle, I neglected to notice the ground was covered in a fine layer of snow.

My feet hit the pavement for only a moment before they were out from under me and I was flat on my back on the tarmac. When I was nine, I fell out of the back of a pickup truck while trying to jump out. My sneaker got caught on the tailgate and long story short, I got a mouth full of dirt. I remember hitting the ground so hard it knocked the breath out of me. The fear of not being able to breathe overlapped the actual pain. At the time, I thought it was the single most embarrassingly painful moment of my life, until now. Falling on a snow-slicked airport tarmac in front of multiple witnesses, including the guy I had once majorly crushed on, was so much worse. Not only because it hurt my ass, which took the brunt of the fall, but my pride took a big punch because falling as an adult is way more embarrassing than when you fall as a child. Plus, the brand-new peacoat I had just bought was getting filthy.

Once I was able to gather myself, I looked up at the many individuals circled around me, who all looked concerned with the exception of one. Grant looked like he was trying not to laugh. I glared up at him, daring him to say anything. His eyes danced with merriment as he reached down to help me up.

"Oh my. Are you okay?" the driver asked from his perch on the last step of the shuttle.

"Fine," I wheezed, looking into Grant's smirking eyes.

"Can you believe she used to be a champion ice skater?" Grant announced loudly, making everyone laugh.

"Oh, that's good. Here, let me give you a round of applause," I said, jerking my hand from his as he helped me to my feet. I lost my footing again and my legs tried sliding out from under me in different directions. Grant reached out and grabbed my jacket just in time to keep me from going down a second time, much to the amusement of everyone watching.

"Hey, I'm not the funny one," he chuckled, keeping a firm hand on my elbow. I would have pulled away, but I wanted to be done embarrassing myself. Only after we entered a large hangar and I was on steady non-slick ground did I jerk my arm from his. His laughter followed me as I made my way down the long rows of purses and suitcases the airline had laid out on the floor. I found my purse quickly, but it took longer to find my small rolling suitcase, which somehow had broken open during the accident. Examining it closer, I could see I wouldn't be able to keep it fastened. Plus, some of my belongings were missing. I sighed, searching for any of my clothing and other personal items. Any loose items had been collectively piled up at the end of the row. Next to the pile was a stack of large plastic bags from Walt Disney World. I laughed at the phrase "The place where dreams come true," along with the image of Mickey Mouse printed on the bag like he was mocking me. Picking through the pile of unclaimed belongings until I was satisfied I had found everything I remembered packing, I transferred everything from my broken suitcase and my stuff I found in the pile into one of the plastic Disney bags.

    Grant was waiting by the hangar door, where a security guard double-checked my belongings, making sure I wasn't taking someone else's luggage. I obliged him, but I wasn't in the mood anymore. I had enough of the airport and was ready to leave now that I had my stuff. After watching him paw through the plastic bag for a moment, my aggravation got the best of me and I spoke up. "Why don't you tell me what you're looking for and I can find it. Or maybe it's still in the plane I was in that crashed," I said sarcastically.

    "Have a nice evening, ma'am," he said, looking unfazed.

"Yeah," I returned as I walked away.

"Everything okay?" Grant asked, plucking the bag off my arm.

"I can carry it," I protested as he slid it onto his shoulder.

"You have more important things to worry about. Like not slipping," he joked as we left the warmth of the hangar. The shuttle bus was waiting to take us back to the terminal. At least the driver had parked closer, and hopefully I wouldn't mortify myself by busting my ass again.

"I figured we can try to get a car from Enterprise when we get back to the terminal, and then maybe look into the rooms the airline is providing at the airport hotel," Grant said conversationally, like everything was set in stone. I opened my mouth to argue, but reason held me back. He was right. It made sense for us to drive together. We were headed to the same destination.

"Fine," I grudgingly agreed, sinking back in my seat while we waited for the shuttle to fill up with more passengers. I was mentally exhausted and sick of all the waiting. Today felt endless. I couldn't believe everything that had happened in the span of ten hours. My body was dragging like I had run a marathon. Not to mention my stomach was threatening mutiny. I hadn't eaten anything substantial since I left my apartment at the crack of dawn. Digging through my purse, I located my phone and pulled it out. I refrained from kissing it since Grant was watching me. Instead, I opened my blog to make sure there was nothing pressing I needed to take care of. After I was reassured my blog would survive until morning, I hit the tab for my Facebook fan page. Scrolling through my notifications, I responded to anything that required my immediate attention before doing a longwinded status update about my day's mishaps. I was ready to post when the sound of a throat being cleared pulled my attention from my phone. Glancing up, I saw the shuttle was empty with the exception of the driver and Grant, who were both studying me like I was an insect or something. I didn't even flush at their looks. It was no secret that when I was in the middle of work-related activities, I could become a bit involved. It was a long-standing joke with everyone who knew me.

"Plan on sleeping here tonight?" Grant asked wryly as the driver looked on with annoyance.

"Sure, can you fetch me a blanket?" I answered, grabbing my bag. I kept my phone in my hand. I didn't need it, but holding it gave me comfort.

Grant rolled his eyes, but didn't seem bothered. The driver, on the other hand, looked pretty disgusted with my phone dependency, but he was an old-timer who probably didn't have a smart phone. I trailed behind Grant as he carried our bags toward the Enterprise counter to rent a car for the following day. I grinned when he requested something with plenty of legroom. At six foot plus, his request totally made sense. Once we had all our paperwork in order for the car, we headed for the airport hotel. I was seriously dragging by the time we approached the desk together.

The desk clerk smiled condescendingly before telling us all the rooms had been taken for the evening.

It took me a moment to register her words since I was dead on my feet. "But we have vouchers," I said, plunking the paper down on the counter like it was a golden ticket to Wonka's chocolate factory.

"Those are only good if there are rooms available. We had a hiccup with an airline earlier today, which resulted in delays with every carrier.

Really, it's to be expected after that kind of chaos," she chirped like she was telling us something we should have already known.

"Hiccup? Is that what they're calling it?" I squawked out. "I think 'hold on to your asses because you're all going to die' would be a more accurate description."

Grant chuckled next me as the smile slipped from the clerk's face as she gaped at me.

"Sorry, I'm just tired," I said more to Grant than the woman who was doing a pretty good impersonation of a guppy.

"No biggie. We'll grab our rental and get a room at another hotel," he reassured me, lifting our bags off the ground.

"Oh, every hotel within a ten-mile radius is completely booked," the clerk, who I was seriously thinking of strangling, said in the same annoyingly chipper tone.

My eyes narrowed as I opened my mouth to tell her where she could shove her chipper tone. Grant grabbed me by the hand and dragged me away from the counter before I could strangle her with the keys she wore around her neck. "She was about to get choked by that freaking scarf around her neck," I grumbled as we staggered back to the Enterprise counter.

"I thought you were going to put her face through her computer monitor," Grant said, chuckling again.

"That would have worked too," I said, sitting on one of the round couches near the Enterprise counter while Grant collected the keys to our rental. I leaned against the back of the couch, closing my eyes briefly. I must have drifted off because the next thing I knew, Grant was shaking me, looking slightly aggravated.

"What's the matter?" I yawned.

"It would seem their car supply is also depleted," he said, sounding as exasperated as I had felt when we found out there were no hotel rooms available.

"And the hits keep on coming," I muttered under my breath.

Chapter 4

"What does that mean?" I asked, afraid the couch I was sitting on would be my temporary bed for the night. Talk about a colossal sucky day.

"It means we have to take what they have available," he grumbled, striding out of the terminal. This time it was my turn to laugh. I was relieved I wouldn't be sleeping in the airport, but it was pretty hilarious to see the normally easygoing Grant losing his cool.

We boarded the rental car company's shuttle and my laughter quickly turned into one yawn after another. The swaying motion of the shuttle bus combined with the snow falling outside lulled me back into my lethargic state. Something about watching snow dropping from the sky had always given me a warm, cozy feeling. It would have been a perfect time to curl up in bed with a good book and hot chocolate.

The shuttle driver stopped in front of what was literally the only car left on the lot. Teeny tiny would be the best way to describe it. I couldn't help barking out in laughter after finally understanding the source of Grant's aggravation. It wasn't one of those Smart Cars, but it was pretty darn close.

"Not funny," Grant declared, wheeling his suitcase through the snow toward the car that looked smaller and smaller the closer he got to it. "I've seen riding lawn mowers with more room than this thing."

I burst out laughing again. He glared at me for a moment before his frown turned to a smile. Even Grant couldn't help laughing at the irony of the situation. A frigid gust of wind blew across the parking lot, sending a shiver down my body. The soft flakes of snow swirled around, pelting my face.

"Here, can you warm up the car?" he asked, handing me the keys while he stowed the luggage in what was supposed to be the trunk.

Only when I was sitting behind the steering wheel of our micro car did the humor of its size lose its luster. We would be cramped driving five miles in this sardine can. Nine hundred plus miles was going to suck. Even with only two of us in the car, we would be practically on top of each other. This was going to be as close to torture as I had ever come.

"I would have driven," Grant said, shaking the snow off his head as he opened the passenger door.

My eyes focused on the stray lock of hair that fell across his forehead. He had great hair for a guy. It was auburn with a lush fullness that would make most girls jealous. I would be embarrassed to admit how often I had dreamed about running my fingers through it.

I reluctantly forced myself to look away. I could NOT fall for Grant again. He had already unknowingly broken my heart once. I would be wise to remember that. Who cares if we were only thirteen years old? A broken heart was a broken heart. Besides, he aggravated the crap out of me, which meant he wasn't Mr. Right.

Oblivious to the jumbled thoughts in my head, Grant adjusted his seat, sliding it as far back as it would go before he climbed in. Even still, his knees were practically in his lap.

"I feel like I'm on a kiddie ride," he complained, adjusting the incline of the seat to try to gain a little more comfort.

"Make sure to keep your arms and legs in the vehicle at all times," I teased, plugging my phone into the charger so I could use the GPS on my phone without draining the battery. Once I selected "Home" from my favorites list, Mona (the name I gave the robotic voice on my phone), started spouting out directions.

"I figured I'd drive until we hit the next town since Ms. Personality claimed the hotels around here are all booked," I told Grant as I drove away from the airport.

"Sounds good," he said, shifting in his seat as I pulled onto the main road. I drove for less than a mile when I turned my blinker on.

"I hope a drive-thru is okay?" I asked, turning into the parking lot of a popular fast food chain.

"That's fine," he said as I pulled behind a heavy-duty truck that dwarfed our small car. The line moved fast and soon we were back on the road. Grant had the juggling act of passing me my food while trying to eat his own, but neither of us wanted to go inside the restaurant. I started to feel more human after I downed my burger and fries. I switched lanes until I was farthest to the left, which I considered my comfort lane. Like the parking lot at Enterprise, the highway was pretty much empty except for an occasional oversized semi-truck.

"This is comfy," Grant said, stowing our trash in the minuscule backseat. He shifted his legs to a suitable position, which happened to be intimately close to my right leg. I debated moving, but that would have been obvious, and possibly lead to an awkward conversation. Instead, I tried to ignore the voice in my head telling me how good his leg felt against mine.

Neither of us talked as the city lights faded away and the night swallowed our lone vehicle. I kept my eyes on the road ahead of me, afraid if I looked at Grant it would start a conversation. It's not like I didn't want to talk to him. I just felt our current driving arrangement was intimate enough without initiating a conversation in the cloak of darkness. A part of me wished he would go to sleep so I could relax a little.

"Are you okay driving?" he asked, making me jump. In all my deep thoughts of not wanting a conversation, I wasn't ready when he initiated one.

"I'm good for now. I'm hoping we'll find a decent hotel there," I said around a yawn as I pointed to a gas station billboard stating the next exit was in twenty-five miles. Despite how tired I was, I felt I could make it.

"Okay. I'd offer to drive, but I'm not sure I'd be able to fit behind that steering wheel," he said sardonically. "Maybe if there's an Enterprise in town we can look into trading this thing for something bigger in the morning."

"I'm okay driving," I said, yawning again. Once the yawns started, there was no stopping. "I drive all the time for work," I added.

"You're some kind of chef, right?" he asked, draping his arm across the back of my seat. If there was something that would wake me up, that was it.

"Um, yeah, but I run a cooking blog," I said, shifting uncomfortably. Grant acted like he didn't notice and continued to talk.

"That's cool. What's your blog called?"

I mumbled the title under my breath.

"Sorry, can you repeat that?" he asked, sounding amused.

"Cooking for Love."

He chuckled. "Still hung up on that whole *love* thing, I see," he observed.

I flushed slightly. I knew my reasons for leaving Woodfalls were common knowledge. I couldn't expect anything less from our small town. "What's wrong with wanting love?" I asked defensively as I maneuvered around a semi-truck that seemed to be having a hard time staying in its own lane. As we passed, I could see the driver was texting on his phone. What an idiot.

"There's nothing wrong with love. You've just always been a bit obsessive about it."

"Obsessive?" I asked in a slightly raised voice that bounced off the tight quarters of the vehicle. "I don't see anything wrong with wanting to find my soul mate," I argued.

His laughter boomed through the vehicle. "Did you say soul mate?" he asked, trying to catch his breath.

"What's wrong with that?" I bristled.

"It's just so cliché, believing there's only one perfect person out there for you. True love is a give-and-take relationship that takes years to perfect," he stated.

"Well, thank you, Dr. Phil. Are you a love therapist now?" I snapped. My faith that my perfect match was somewhere out there had been keeping me going for so long. It was the whole reason I traveled so much for my job. I have this fantasy of walking into a romantic restaurant and waiting at the bar for my table. The bartender sets down a glass of red wine and points to a tall, dark and handsome gentleman at the other end of the bar who raises his glass when I look in his direction. He walks over confidently and introduces himself. The connection is instantaneous. We have dinner together and talk all night long until we share the most passionate kiss ever as the sun rises in the horizon and we have our happily ever after. It could happen.

"Nope. I read it on the back of a cereal box," he quipped. I elbowed him in his ribs, but he deserved it. I hated that I was always the butt of his jokes.

"Hey, kidding. I learned it from watching my parents all these years. They love each other deeply, but that's because they're willing to put the work into their relationship. You can't just expect to have some love fairy wave her magic wand and *poof*, you've met your soul mate," he said sarcastically. He removed his arm from the back of my seat and I couldn't help feeling like he was mad at me or something, which was utterly ridiculous. If anyone should be pissed it was me.

I stewed on his words, not saying anything for the next ten miles. When another billboard appeared declaring we were two miles from our gas needs (their words, not mine), I let out a small sigh of relief. I was ready to get out of the car and put some space between us. I had no idea how I was going to handle the rest of the trip when the first hour had pretty much done me in.

Grant must have felt the same since he looked relieved when our exit came into view. Merging onto the off-ramp, I followed the signs to the only hotel in the area.

"Roach motel, anyone?" Grant said as I pulled into the parking lot that was in dire need of some repairs, but seemed to be the least of their problems. The office had an illuminated sign, but the first few letters were burned out, so all it said was "fice."

"Are we sure it hasn't been condemned?" I said with dismay. I was by no means a snob, but I did expect a certain degree of cleanliness when I stayed in a hotel. Hopefully, it had fresh sheets and towels and clean floors, and not to knock this place any more, but I would prefer it if the night manager wasn't picking his nose as we walked in the front door.

"You folks like a room?" he asked, chewing on his thumbnail that had just been in his nose. Double gag.

"Are there any other hotels in the area?" I asked hopefully as Grant snickered.

"No, ma'am. We here have the only accommodations in a twenty-mile radius," he said proudly, spitting a section of his nail off to the side.

"Charming," I replied.

"Two rooms," Grant said, stepping in before I had the chance to say anything more.

"Two? I thought you two were *together,*" he said, looking at me with a whole new level of interest.

"We are," Grant glared at him. "We'd like our rooms to be adjoining," he added.

The clerk shrugged his shoulders after eyeing me up and down one last time before giving us our total. My skin crawled, but I ignored him as I paid for both rooms. Grant tried to intervene, but I reminded him that he had paid for the car. With one last wink from Mr. Nose Picker, I grabbed our two room keys and walked out of the office. Grant stood for a moment with his fist clenched before turning around to follow me out.

"Bit of a creep, huh?" I said as I climbed back into the car to drive us to the end of the building where our rooms were located.

"Dickhead is more like it," Grant answered.

As we climbed from the car and grabbed our bags, I was almost thankful it was so dark outside. If I saw the building in the harsh light of day, I'm not sure I could have forced myself to stay.

Grant waited beside me while I slid the key into the lock and twisted the handle. The strong stench of old mildewed carpet assaulted my senses when I pushed the door open. Reaching a hand along the wall, I found the light switch and turned it on. Swallowing hard, I stepped into the room, which was far worse than I imagined. The carpet was worn with the concrete floor exposed in several areas. What there was of carpet was stained. By what, I didn't even want to think about. The walls that were once white were a dingy yellow from years of neglect and cigarette smoke discoloration. There was a bed and a small dresser with a broken leg that made it wobble when you touched it.

"I'm in hell," I mumbled, walking farther into the room. I was afraid to touch anything else and didn't know how I was going to manage sleeping here.

"Well, that's not true. If it was hell, it wouldn't be this damn cold," Grant said, walking over to my thermostat to adjust the heat. A groaning noise moved through the wall, but thankfully a blast of warm air blew through the vent. "I guess I better go check if mine is any better," he added, opening the door that adjoined our rooms. The second door was warped and didn't close completely.

"I guess it's a good thing you're the one in the room adjacent to mine," I said sarcastically as he pushed the warped door open, which creaked loudly.

"On a positive note, you can rest well knowing I can't sneak up on you," he said, making the door squeak again as he walked into his room.

I circled around again to take in the room, unsure of what I wanted to do. I was dead tired, but my day of travel had left me feeling frumpy and dirty. Standing in the middle of my disgusting room wasn't helping matters. Still holding my bag, I stripped off the comforter that looked like it hadn't been washed in a decade. The sheets looked marginally better. After giving them a quick inspection, I figured they would have to do. I placed my bag and purse on the middle of the bed and headed to the bathroom with a pair of socks and my bathroom bag in hand. I paused along the way to close the door that separated our adjoining rooms.

I showered quickly, in part because I could barely keep my eyes open, but mostly because the hot water worked about as well as everything else at the motel. Drying off, I pulled on my socks, since there was no way I was walking on the floor with bare feet. The towels were small and barely wrapped around my torso. I had to admit, as tired as I felt, the bed suddenly didn't look as bad as it had a few minutes ago. I decided to lie down for a minute to see how the mattress felt. My intention was to get back up and put on some pajamas, but before I knew it, my eyes closed and I was out.

***

I was having one of those half in-half out kinds of dreams when a tickling sensation on my leg caused me to stir. I tried to ignore it, not wanting to wake up. It was only when the tickling moved up my leg that my mind sprang to awareness. With speed that would make a track star envious, I leaped from the bed, screaming bloody murder. Swatting at my thigh, I knocked the biggest bug I had ever seen from my body just as Grant charged into my room. He looked like a wild man ready for action with a lamp clutched in his hand. Despite my bug phobia, it didn't escape my notice that Grant was wearing nothing but boxer briefs that left little to the imagination. It was at that moment that I remembered I had neglected to put on pajamas before I fell asleep. My eyes met Grant's as he came to two obvious conclusions at once. One—I wasn't being attacked by some mass murderer, and two—I was standing in the middle of the room stark naked with the exception of my Care Bears socks.

Chapter 5

Grant's eyes drifted from my face down to my very naked body. Grabbing the towel at my feet, I hastily wrapped it around my torso, which didn't cover much since the towel was intended for a child.

"What the hell are you doing? Don't look!" I yelled while attempting to cover all the important areas.

Grant's expression sparkled with a mixture of amusement and desire. My knees suddenly felt weak as a flush tinted my cheeks.

"I thought someone was murdering you," he laughed, dragging his eyes away from my breasts, which could still be seen through my clenched fists that were trying to hold up the towel.

"It was a bug," I screeched as the offending insect crawled across the floor. Without any thought of the consequences, I flew across the room into Grant's arms.

Perhaps it would have been erotic if I wasn't trying to climb him like a monkey.

"As nice as it feels to have you...wrapped around me, if you want me to kill your little friend, you're going to have to let go," he said in strained voice. Releasing him self-consciously, I realized I had stepped over the line. He was seeing someone. Sure, he had been nice to me all day, and at times even flirty, but that was probably just me trying to fabricate something that wasn't there. It didn't help the situation to think about how good his rock-hard bare chest felt pressed against mine, or how low his boxers fit on his hips.

"Sorry," I said, untangling my arms from around his neck. I stepped away from him as he picked up one of my boots and held it in the air. "Wait, don't use my boot," I pleaded, but I was too late. The crunching sound made me grimace even though I was glad the bug was gone.

"Nice socks," he said, wiping the sole of my boot on the carpet.

"Thanks," I squeaked. He walked to my bathroom and came back a moment later with a wad of toilet paper. I wanted to gag when he scooped up the dead bug carcass and flushed it down the toilet.

My heart rate returned to normal now that the threat was gone. Of course, the fact that Grant had not only seen my goods, but that I had also thrown myself into his arms like some damsel in distress was still hanging out there. No pun intended to myself. I pawed through my bag and found my PJ shorts and sleeping shirt before heading to the bathroom. For future reference, I will make sure I get dressed before going to sleep from now on.

After a pity party that abruptly ended when I saw another bug crawl out from under the sink, I left the bathroom. We were literally in the roach hell motel.

Grant was still standing in the doorway of our adjoining rooms looking at me like I had been dipping in spiked eggnog.

"What? I hate bugs. Okay?" I said, surveying the room like I expected an army of roaches to appear at any moment to drag me away.

"I'm just disappointed you decided to put on some clothes. That'll take half the fun out of coming back in here if you see another one," he said, dropping my boot and heading back to his room.

"Glad you enjoyed the show," I said, playing along, although my adrenaline was rushing through my veins.

When I was able to clear the image of his six-pack from my mind, I looked around at all the possible places a bug could hide. I debated going to the car to sleep, but the thought of freezing my butt off held me back. This was officially shaping up to be the worst holiday season ever. I should have followed my instincts and opted for a sandy beach instead. It was too late to cry over spilled milk, so I came up with a plan where I could hopefully get a little sleep. I started off by pulling the bed away from the wall. Thankfully it wasn't bolted down like everything else in the room. Once the bed was as far away from the walls as I could get it, I stripped it to make sure there were no more unwanted guests hiding in the sheets. After shaking them out, I replaced the fitted sheet on the bed and wrapped the remaining sheet around my body papoose style so nothing could crawl up my bare legs again. Only after I tucked my head under the sheet did I feel somewhat safe from any more creepy crawlies. I left the light on and fell into an uneasy sleep that involved dreams with naked chests covered in bugs.

Scratching noises on the ceiling above woke me the next morning as I emerged from the safety of my sheet cocoon. I pulled my head out in time to see two roaches scurrying across the ceiling right toward the bed. Biting back a screech, I jumped off my bed, not thinking about the sheet that was tightly wrapped around my body. Twice in two days I found myself flat on my back with the breath knocked out of my lungs. Hell. If this wasn't Christmas hell, I don't know what was.

"I'm not sure I would have picked the floor to sleep on," Grant said as his face came into view. "It looks a little rough down there."

"Bite me," I wheezed, struggling to my feet. One thing was clear; I couldn't have done a better job wrapping myself in the sheet. With it tangled around my legs, I pitched forward, landing directly in Grant's arms.

"You've gotten pretty forward with age," Grant teased, wrapping his hands around my biceps to steady me. "I mean, biting you doesn't sound like that bad of an idea, but we should probably build up to that."

"Very funny," I snapped. It was aggravating that I couldn't seem to get my act together when he was around. When I finally managed to untangle the sheet from my legs, I threw it across the room in a fit of anger. It fluttered harmlessly to the floor, taking the oomph out of my action.

Grant threw his head back, laughing loudly. Ignoring him, I stomped off to the bathroom only to return a moment later for my boot. Six smashed bugs later, I was dressed and ready to leave the roach motel behind.

By the time Grant joined me, I was already in the car with the engine running. He refrained from commenting as I tore out of the parking lot like the hounds of hell were after us. Twenty seconds later, I was muttering every swear word I knew under my breath when flashing lights showed up in my rearview mirror. "Not a word," I told Grant, who was smirking. I glared at him, even though I was more pissed at myself. Go figure, I'd get my first-ever speeding ticket now. This was the cherry on top of the crap sundae these last few days had been. I rested my head on the steering wheel and counted to ten so I wouldn't lose my shit with the approaching highway patrolman.

Grant kept his mouth zipped as the officer wrote me a ticket for going fifty in a thirty-five mile-per-hour zone. My teeth ground together as he called me "young lady" and pointed out that maybe I should leave the driving to my boyfriend. The temptation to drive the vehicle over his condescending ass was strong, but I could only imagine what jail would have in store for me with the luck I'd been having. After fifteen minutes of being reprimanded on safe driving, the sexist, asshole cop finally let us go. I left the odious town behind, clenching the steering wheel in a death grip. To Grant's credit, he kept his mouth closed. I swear if he would have commented, or if I would have seen so much as a smirk on his face, he would have been walking home.

    Fifty miles of silence later, I finally cut my eyes over at Grant. "Are you hungry?" I asked.

    "Oh, hello. Am I allowed to talk?" he asked, sounding amused.

    "My humiliation is a never-ending source of entertainment for you, isn't it? Has there ever been a time when I wasn't doing something you could make fun of?" I complained, taking the next exit that boasted several restaurants. Without asking for his preference, I pulled into the parking lot of a quaint-looking diner.

    "Making fun? Is that what you think I've been doing?" he asked, unfolding his six-foot-plus frame from the car. He groaned as he worked the kinks out of his body. "I swear, riding in a coffin would be more comfortable," he complained, bending over to stretch his back. I expected him to elaborate on why I thought he'd been teasing me our entire lives, but he continued to whine about the size of the car as we made our way into the diner. The air outside was brisk. I shivered, staring up at the low hanging clouds in the sky. I had lived in a snowy state long enough to know when a bad storm was coming.

The warm restaurant, on the other hand, was absolutely heavenly. "Wow, I think an elf threw up in here," I said sarcastically. It's not that I hated Christmas decorations. All the rotten luck over the past couple of days had just made me overly cranky.

"I think they're cool," Grant said, taking in the endless array of mismatched Christmas decorations covering every available wall space. There were multiple Nativity scenes and each one seemed to be missing pieces. I couldn't help wondering why they didn't combine them into one complete set. It was impossible to count the number of Santa Clauses scattered around, but I did spot five Christmas trees in varying sizes. Whoever decorated them had quite the sense of humor. The funniest one was decorated using different beer cans as ornaments.

"How many?" an elderly waitress asked, looking up from a table she was wiping down.

"Two," Grant and I answered in unison.

"Aww, aren't you two so cute," she said, grabbing two menus from the hostess stand. "My husband and I used to be in sync like that. Of course, now he's too busying fiddling around in his workshop to be in sync with anything else." She winked at me conspiratorially. Neither Grant nor I bothered to correct her assumption that we were a couple since she had already moved on to another topic. In the short walk to our booth, we learned she had been married thirty years and had two daughters that now lived out of state. Grant grinned at me as she placed our menus on a table that sat in front of the long bank of windows that looked out the front of the restaurant.

"I'm surprised you two lovebirds decided to venture out. That storm is going to be a doozy," she said, placing two filled water glasses on our table as the first snowflakes began to fall from the sky.

I kicked Grant's leg when he snorted over her choice of words. "We're just passing through," I answered.

She shook her head before I finished getting the words out. "I'm not sure that's the best idea. This storm is supposed to stretch across six counties. I guess if you have four-wheel drive you might be able to make a go of it," she commented, glancing out the window.

Grant and I looked at each other, trying not to laugh. The only way we would have four-wheel drive was if we picked up our matchbox car and placed it in the bed of the nearest Ford truck.

"I'm thinking you'll be with us the next few days," she chirped cheerily, obviously thinking the same thing. "Now what can I get you to drink?"

"Coffee," Grant answered.

"I'll take the same," I answered, peering out the window. I was distracted by the snow that was already falling harder. There was no way we could be stuck here for two days. We were still more than seven hundred miles from Woodfalls, and Christmas was in four days. My mom would have my head if I didn't make it there for all the pre-Christmas festivities.

"Don't worry, I'm sure this storm isn't as bad as she's making it," Grant said like he had read my mind. I pulled my eyes from the window and saw that he was studying me as intently as I had been studying the falling snow.

"I hope not. My mom will kill me if I don't make it home for Christmas," I mumbled, fidgeting with my spoon on the table.

"I'll get you home," he said confidently, sitting back in his chair.

"Oh, you'll be driving?" I teased.

"When I say 'I'll get you home,' I mean more figuratively," he answered.

"Thought so." I smiled as June, our waitress, came back with two steaming cups of coffee. She took our food order after telling us she had called her niece who runs a bed and breakfast and told her that we'd be coming by.

"Oh, that was nice of you, but I think we're going to see how far we can get," I said, handing her my menu.

Her eyes widened with disbelief, but she didn't say anything as she headed back to the kitchen shaking her head. Not that she gave up. Throughout our meal, she gave us updates on the weather and traffic conditions. She sounded like a walking highway safety billboard as she quoted statistics for weather-related car accidents. She even tried highlighting how lovely and romantic her niece's bed and breakfast was. I thanked her for her concern, but remained adamant that we were continuing on. I explained how our families were expecting us home for the holidays and would be disappointed if we didn't make it. Grant was no help. All he could do was sit and try not to laugh with every recurring visit to the table.

"You were no help," I chastised him as we paid the check.

"I think her concern is sweet," he said as we both shrugged into our jackets.

"I brought you two crazy kids a couple of coffees to go," June said, bustling out of the kitchen. "You come back and see us here in Whisper Hollow when you're not so pressed for time. Next time you'll have to try our waffles and legendary maple syrup. It's the best maple in the state," she boasted.

"We will," I promised, even though there really wasn't a "we" when it came to Grant and me. "Thank you, June," I said, impulsively giving her a hug. Maybe it was the cheesy Christmas decorations or I was touched by how concerned she was, but I felt an odd kinship with her. It made the stay in the roach motel last night that much worse knowing we could have stayed here instead if we had known about it.

Waving at June one last time, Grant and I left the warmth of the restaurant behind. We crunched our way to the car through the layer of snow that was effectively covering the ground.

"Do you want me to drive?" Grant asked. The offer was sweet, but I could see him eyeing the compact space behind the steering wheel skeptically.

"Don't worry about it, big boy. I got it," I teased, easily sliding my petite frame behind the wheel.

"Take it slow and easy," he directed as I pulled out of the parking lot and merged onto the highway.

I shot him a look that said I knew how to drive, even though I heeded his advice and let up on the accelerator a bit. The car still shimmied and slid on the slick highway. We didn't have a lot of weight in this small car. I let up on the accelerator a bit more as the snow fell even heavier. Our progress was slow, and I was beginning to think June was right. Only someone crazy would be driving on this road.

Without warning, the car lost traction. I barely had time to react as we slid sideways across the highway. Luckily, no cars were coming from the opposite direction. I removed my foot from the accelerator and stayed off the brakes. Thankfully, I had some experience driving on icy roads. I knew to turn the wheel in the opposite direction of our skid to keep the car from spinning around, but as much as I tried, we continued to slide sideways and down the short embankment. The car protested with a loud grinding noise and came to a jarring halt in a narrow gully off the side of the road.

Chapter 6

"Well, hell, that was fun," I muttered, gripping the steering wheel with shaking hands. The car was no longer running, but smoke was seeping out from under the hood.

"Are you okay?" Grant asked. I had a strange sense of déjà vu. Just yesterday he had asked me the same question after the plane crash.

"Yeah, but I'm starting to feel like we're in one of those *Final Destination* movies," I said, resting my head against the steering wheel. The vehicle shook slightly from Grant's laughter. As always, I was so glad I was here to amuse him.

"It's not funny," I stated, although my own lips began to quirk from watching him trying to hold his laughter in check.

"You're like the ultimate traveling bad luck charm," Grant said, between howls of laughter.

"Me? How do you know it's not you? I've never had this much trouble getting from one place to the other before," I said as my own laughter rippled through me. I guess under the circumstances, it was good that we had a sense of humor over our experience. It would definitely give us a story to tell.

"We better head back to Whisper Hollow," Grant said as the snow continued to fall.

"Seriously? How far do you think we've gone?" I wasn't relishing a walk along the highway in my designer boots that were designed more for fashion than function.

"It's probably less than five miles. If we're lucky, we can get back to town before the sun sets. Besides, what choice do we have? Look at your phone. There's no signal out here."

Terrific. Five miles might not seem like a big deal to him, but for someone like me, who avoided exercise like the plague, five miles might as well be ten miles. "Maybe we should wait for someone to drive by and help," I offered hopefully.

"Did I miss all the traffic driving by? I think this is rush hour. Even if a car does happen to be out in these conditions, there's no guarantee they'd stop for us. We could wind up waiting and then be stuck here all night. I don't know about you, but sleeping in this tuna can is not my idea of a fun time," he said. He pulled on the handle of his door to climb out, but it wouldn't budge. "Damn it," he grumbled. "It's stuck. You're going to have to climb out first and then I'll go out your side," he said, looking at the center console and steering wheel apprehensively.

"I can't wait to see this," I spurted out, laughing. It was almost worth the five-mile walk for him to finally be the butt of the joke. Almost.

Five minutes and multiple swear words, bumps and more swear words later, Grant and I were headed back the way we had come, this time on foot. Grant carried the recyclable Disney bag I had gotten from the airport that now contained a change of clothes for each of us and the necessary toiletries. I carried my purse with all our gadgets. He tried to talk me into leaving my laptop behind, thinking it would become dead weight, but I refused. My laptop was my life. I would drag my purse behind me through the snow before I left my laptop. I could tell he wanted to argue further, but he just shook his head, mumbling something about priorities. He didn't seem to get that my job was a priority and my laptop was a tool I needed.

I threw one last wistful look at the car that was already covered by a thin layer of snow. Pretty soon it would match the cover on the ground, which was up to my ankles. At first, I was okay walking along. It was kind of nice to have the snow floating down around us. Even as cold as I was at first, after twenty minutes of brisk walking while trying not to slip, I had warmed up and was tempted to take off my jacket. Once the wind kicked up, it was a different story. Neither Grant nor I talked as we trudged forward with the swirling snow whipping into our faces. Grant stuck close to me, lending a hand when the soles of my boots caused me to slip.

Forty minutes into our journey, I finally broke the silence. "So, what do you do for a living now?" I asked, huffing slightly in the brisk air. I had been dying to know what he had been up to since I left Woodfalls. I was just always too afraid to ask. He may think I'm crazy for asking now, but it was a way to pass the time.

"I took over for my dad at the lumber yard. He still comes in every day, but he basically turned over the day-to-day responsibilities to me when I graduated," Grant answered, not sounding nearly as winded as I was.

"Wow, that's great. I was afraid after the fires in '09 the plant was going to have to close," I admitted.

My father had kept me abreast on what was going on while I was away at college. It was all he could talk about every time I called home. He was worried and rightfully so. He had been the shift manager at the plant for twenty years. The lumberyard was his life. He wasn't the only one. Half the population in Woodfalls had ties to the plant in one capacity or another.

"That was a tough year, but I helped out whenever I wasn't in class. There was some rebuilding that needed to be done, but everyone really pulled together," Grant said.

"That's Woodfalls," I said nostalgically. "Whisper Hollow kind of reminds me of Woodfalls," I added. He nodded his head in agreement and I felt a wave of homesickness. In the four and half years I'd been gone, I had only returned for short stints, mostly around the holidays. It was the seasons I missed the most. Like the fall when the leaves changed colors in September and early October. The landscape would be a painter's canvas of yellow, red and orange. Spring was equally enchanting as new life bloomed in the plants that had been dormant all winter.

"Sounds like you miss it," he said, looking at me with surprise.

"Of course I miss it," I said halting. "Woodfalls is my home."

He also stopped. "You could have fooled me. You hightailed it out of there almost the moment we graduated and never looked back," he added, sounding aggravated, although I couldn't imagine why. His steps were longer than before, as if he was trying to outdistance his sudden annoyance with me.

"I had things I needed to do," I stated, stalking after him as my own anger rose. What was it to him that I had been gone for a while? It's not like we were friends or anything before I left. My own aggravation made me forget to watch my step on the uneven snow-covered path. I was practically running to keep up with him when my right foot stepped into a hole that was covered in snow. My ankle buckled and the forward momentum carried me to a heap on the ground with a cry of pain. The throbbing in my ankle outweighed the fact that I had fallen in front of Grant again. I chanted a few words that would have made a sailor blush as I extracted my foot from the booby trap it had stepped in.

Without hesitation, Grant dropped the bag he was carrying so he could kneel in front of me. "Are you okay?" he asked me for the third time in two days as he wiped away a tear that rolled down my cheek.

"I'm not sure," I answered, pulling my pant leg up to inspect the damage. My boot was covering my throbbing ankle. I made a move to take it off, but Grant stopped me.

"You better keep it on. If your ankle is swelling you might not be able to get it back on," he said, looking worried.

"How much farther you think?" I asked, squinting in the snow that was falling more rapidly.

"Two miles, give or take," he said, reaching a hand out to help me up. Grasping my hand tightly, he helped me to my feet. The instant I put weight on my leg it bucked and I bit back another cry of pain.

"Mother sucking of all bad luck," I grunted, hobbling on my one good foot.

Grant looked back the way we had just come and then back to the way we still needed to go. Go figure. Only I would hurt my ankle at exactly the halfway point.

"We have to keep going. It's okay. I'm going to help you," he said, effortlessly scooping me up into his arms.

"Wait, you can't carry me," I squirmed.

"Well, I don't want to freeze my ass off out here, and this is probably faster than helping you limp the rest of the way," he said, adjusting me snugly against his chest. His rock-hard chest I might add. "I'm going to have to leave the bag. I'll have to get it later," he said, striding toward town.

I cradled my purse in my arms, feeling guilty that he was supporting my weight along with our stuff, but we had no choice. Our phones and my computer would never make it covered in snow. My throbbing ankle continued to make its presence known, but I wasn't going to lie, his arms felt absolutely dreamy wrapped around me. Without giving any conscious thought to it, I snuggled closer. He responded by tightening his arms more securely. It had been longer than I would care to admit since I had been held intimately like this. My last relationship was a disaster to say the least. We fizzled out quickly when I realized the guy I had been dating basically lied to me about everything from his job, where he went to school, where he lived. Turns out he had dropped out of college and was still living at home while he worked odd jobs. I'm still not convinced he had given me his real name. Thankfully, it had only taken me a few dates to see through his load of crap.

I'd like to say my other ventures in the dating world had been more successful, but between Dan the Forever Crotch Grabber and Steve the Perpetual Xbox Gamer, my dating endeavors hadn't been very successful. Long-term relationships never seemed to be in my grasp. I felt like Taylor Swift. Minus all the money, of course.

"Are you still seeing Amanda?" I asked impulsively. The moment the words left my mouth I wished I could have retracted them. Did I really want to know about Amanda at this moment?

"Amanda?" he asked, puzzled. "No, we broke up right after you left."

My pulse felt like it galloped at his words.

"She married Stan last year."

"Oh, wow. I thought you guys were serious," I said, trying not to sound as excited as I felt. His words gave me permission to not feel so guilty for enjoying the way it felt to be held in his arms. The heady scent of his cologne swirled around me. I remembered the smell acutely. All through senior year, this had been his scent choice. Thanks to Ms. Garrison's statistics class and her insistence that we sit in alphabetical order, I had to sit behind Grant the entire year smelling it. Memories from back then flooded my mind and I fought the temptation to bury my face in his neck.

I felt him shrug before he answered. "She wanted things I couldn't give her," he answered.

Great, he had a commitment phobia. "I'm sure she would have waited until you were ready."

"I was never going to be ready," he answered.

Gah, commitment-phobe to the max. All my hopeful feelings from a few seconds ago deflated like a balloon. I wasn't looking for a guy who strings a girl along for four years and then drops her like a hot potato when she wants something more. I get the whole waiting thing, but you had to give a person something. For the first time, I actually felt bad for Amanda. Maybe I had dodged the bullet since Grant was never interested in me.

"I got it. You're a perpetual playboy," I finally analyzed, looking at the falling snow in front of us.

"Playboy? You grew up in Woodfalls, right? I'm not sure there are enough women there to be considered a playboy," he chuckled. "Besides, Fran would have my head," he added.

"How is Fran?" I asked, momentarily distracted. I had fond memories of the woman who owned the small store back home. Where most towns had fast food restaurants where all the teenagers hung out, we had Fran's. She had always welcomed us in no matter how loud we were. She made sure to have our favorite snacks on hand and allowed us to claim the front porch of the store as long as we didn't disrupt the customers coming in and out. The best thing about Fran was that she was never too busy to listen to any of us. I loved my cousin Tressa and we had been close growing up, but once I hit high school, the two-year gap between our ages made it hard for me to talk to her at times. Fran was the only one in Woodfalls who knew about my feelings for Grant. She was my shoulder to cry on, dishing out tissues and advice at the same time. Eventually, I stopped focusing of Grant and told her about my desire to leave Woodfalls so I could meet Mr. Right. Fran was never crazy about the idea and made it her goal to find me the perfect guy in Woodfalls. For months after, I would arrive at her store to find a different guy from school who Fran had somehow convinced to help her with some project she had fabricated. Her plan never worked, but she deserved an A for the effort.

"She's the same. Causing havoc and flirting with all the men in town her age and some who aren't her age. Of course, she's set her sights on Tressa's friend's dad."

"What? Brittni's dad came back?" I asked, completely floored.

"No, not Brittni. Her friend Ashton."

"Ashton? Why don't I remember her in school?"

"You wouldn't. Tressa met Ashton when she was in Woodfalls a couple summers ago. She came back last summer to get married over on the James property."

"Wow, I guess I've missed a lot," I mused, turning my face back around to look at him. I was startled to see he was looking down at me intently. "What?" I asked self-consciously.

"You have something on your nose."

"Oh," I flushed, turning my face away from his. I ran my hand over my nose, completely embarrassed.

"It was just a snowflake," he said, chuckling.

"Creep," I muttered, swatting at his arm.

"So, you plan on returning to Woodfalls anytime soon? I mean, for other than the holidays?" he asked, adjusting me in his arms.

"Not with the rate I'm going," I muttered, keeping my face averted from his.

He started to answer until we both heard a vehicle approaching in the distance. Grant gently stood me up and we waved our arms to get the driver's attention.

Chapter 7

A pickup truck much like June had suggested we needed slowed to a stop on the side of the road. "You folks need some help?" the driver asked after opening his door.

"Yes, sir," Grant answered, walking toward him.

The large burly bear of a man stepped from the truck. He stood easily at six and a half feet tall. Grant was tall, and even he looked miniature next to this stranger. The nickname "Refrigerator" would have suited him well. Dressed in a flannel shirt that was rolled up to reveal massive forearms, he looked like a lumberjack, or in my mind, a serial killer.

"Are you sure this is a good idea?" I asked under my breath. "He might be some crazy mountain-man killer."

"Nah, he has to be cool. He has a Pittsburg Steelers flag in his back window."

"Even more reason not to trust him. Everyone knows the only people you can trust are Bills fans."

"You know football?" Grant asked.

"Um, hello? I was born in Woodfalls," I joked. Football and Woodfalls came as a package. With not a whole lot else to get excited about in a town the size of Woodfalls, football was practically a religion. To say you didn't like football was pretty much sacrilegious, and were considered fighting words. Fridays were spent traveling to high school games since our school didn't have a home field. Saturdays we watched college ball, and Sundays, of course were all about the Buffalo Bills. Even after almost five years away from Woodfalls, football was still in my blood.

"I'm Tim," the stranger introduced himself. "My wife, June, thought you folks might need a hand. She said you had it in your heads to drive some Barbie car in this storm," Tim said, opening the passenger door so Grant could set me down on the seat. My misgivings were put to rest. Of course June sent him out to check on us.

"Barbie car. Ha, that's not far off," Grant laughed, sliding in beside me. I sighed with pleasure at the warm air coming from the vents.

"How long you folks been walking?"

"Just over an hour. I think our car is about three miles up. We slid off the road. Then poor Jamie here stepped in a hole. I'm not sure if she broke her ankle or just sprained it, but we had to leave the bag I was carrying. I'd sure appreciate it if you would let me collect it."

"Not a problem at all. We'll also check on your car."

"That would be wonderful," I said. It would be great to have a change of clothing. I pulled my gloves off so I could hold my hands in front of the vents. I had been so preoccupied in Grant's arms I didn't realize how cold I was.

It took Tim less than two minutes to spot our bag on the side of the road where we had left it. Grant jumped from the vehicle to retrieve it. He brushed off the snow and handed it me to hold on my lap with my purse. When he climbed back into the truck, he was careful not to bump my ankle, which had started throbbing now that it was no longer elevated over his arm.

"Our car should be pretty close from here," Grant said, closing his door hard.

"How's your ankle feel, missy," Tim asked, shifting the truck from first to second gear.

"I'm not sure to tell you the truth, but I know it hurts," I admitted, grimacing.

"I'll bet. Don't worry. Doc Jones will get you fixed up."

Grant and I both burst out laughing. Tim shot us a look like we'd lost our minds.

"Sorry," I said between giggles. "We have a Doc Jones in the town we grew up in. We were just saying how much Whisper Hollow reminds us of home."

"I'll be darned. Small town, huh? Nothing wrong with that," Tim said like we had just declared we were all members of the same secret society. "Would you look at that. She was right. I think my grandkids have remote control cars bigger than that," Tim stated, pulling onto the shoulder of the highway. I was surprised to see our car covered with a blanket of snow that easily was six inches deep. I had no idea the snow had been coming down that hard while we were walking.

"Yeah, it definitely wasn't our first choice, but it was all they had at the airport," Grant replied, climbing from the vehicle. He took the plastic bag with him, saying he would grab the rest of my stuff. I blushed slightly thinking about him seeing the bras and panties I had tried to hide between my sweaters. Hopefully he would leave everything folded and just add it to the bag.

The guys made quick work of grabbing the rest of our things, but by the time Tim turned the truck around, Mother Nature had kicked it up a notch. We were in an all-out blizzard. Even with chains on the tires, Tim had to grip the steering wheel and reduce our speed to a near crawl. We all remained silent so Tim could concentrate on the treacherous conditions. When we finally turned off the highway and drove into the Whisper Hollow town limits, we couldn't have been any more relieved.

"We don't have a hotel here, but our niece runs a real nice bed and breakfast," Tim said, turning down a road a half mile off the exit. The town of Whisper Hollow came into view and the homesickness I had been feeling for Woodfalls returned again. I had fought my mom this year on coming home for Christmas, but at the moment I would do anything to be driving down Main Street in Woodfalls, surrounded by friends and family who all loved me. Instead, I was stuck several states away in a strange town with the last person I would have ever expected to be stranded with.

Whisper Hollow looked to be half the size of Woodfalls, although I'm sure they had their areas that stretched beyond the little town we were driving through. With the blanket of snow covering it, the town resembled something you would see on a Christmas card. Especially since everything was completely decked out for Christmas like the diner had been.

"I'll drop you off here at the B&B first and then send Doc your way," Tim said, pulling behind a large Victorian house with long sweeping porches on the first and second floors. A huge Christmas wreath hung from the highest eve of the house while lighted garland draped the porch railings on both levels.

"Thank you so much. We can't thank you enough," I said to Tim.

"I'm happy to help, darling. Let's get you two inside."

"This is beautiful. Magical," I breathed as Grant opened the truck door and swept me back up into his arms. My eyes met his only to see he was studying me the way he had earlier when he told me I had a snowflake on my nose. I waited for a teasing comment or for him to make some joke since that was his norm, but he did neither. His eyes moved to my lips. Unconsciously, I dragged my bottom lip between my teeth, not wanting to admit how long I had dreamed about what his lips would feel like on mine. I shouldn't want them. He had all but declared that serious relationships weren't for him. Maybe something casual could work. Just this once.

Tim interrupted the moment when he rounded the vehicle carrying our bags. I wasn't sure if I was relieved or disappointed. With me tucked into his arms, Grant trailed behind Tim as they climbed the four shallow steps to the front porch.

A bell chimed above the front door as Tim pushed it open. The foyer opened up to reveal a large grand staircase that greeted us as we stepped into the warm space that smelled like cinnamon and sugar cookies.

"Uncle Tim, what are you doing out in a storm like this?" a plump, pleasant-looking woman who looked to be in her early thirties asked, stepping into the foyer.

"Hey, Mags. These kind folks here ran into some trouble with the storm. Do you have any rooms available? I know you have that crew here from Georgia who come every year, but I thought maybe you could squeeze 'em in," Tim said, sliding his arms around his niece's shoulder. "Grant and Jamie, this is my niece, Maggie. Or Mags to those of us who watched her grow up from being a peanut. Maggie, this is Grant and Jamie." He finished the introductions with a nod in our direction.

"It's nice to meet you two. I expected to see you earlier after Aunt June called today," she said, reaching out to shake our hands, which was a bit awkward since I was still in Grant's arms. "You're in luck. I had a cancellation on the Washington room," she said, wiping her hands on her Christmas apron that was covered in flour. "Are you on your honeymoon?" she asked, probably wondering why Grant hadn't put me down yet.

Her question was simple enough to answer, but for some reason, it suddenly felt like the white elephant in the room. I dared not look at Grant, afraid of the mocking that was sure to be there. Knowing him, he'd come up with some kind of joke at my expense. To beat him to the punch, I jumped in with the first thing that popped into my head. "Hell no," I all but shouted, hearing myself echo in the small foyer. An uncomfortable silence filled the room and I wouldn't have blamed Grant if he dropped me on my ass.

"I mean, I hurt my ankle," I finally said, finding the rational answer. "That's why my *friend* Grant is carrying me."

"Oh, you poor thing. Let me show you up to your room," she said, grabbing an old-fashioned looking key off an elegant key rack that hung next to the small reception desk. "Do you want me to call Doc Jones, or are you going to go get him?" she asked Tim.

"I'm going to fetch him. That ole pickup truck of his has been giving him some issues. I keep telling him it's time to drive to the city to get a new model. You know him though. He feels if he fiddles with it a little, it'll be good as new."

"That's Doc for ya. He feels there ain't nothing broken that can't be fixed," Maggie told us with twinkling eyes as she headed for the staircase. "I'll get these two settled in then," she threw over her shoulder.

Grant followed behind her with me still tucked in his arms, which I was thankful for. After my slip of the tongue, he could have left me in a heap at the bottom of the stairs.

Maggie led us down a long hallway, stopping at the last door at the end of the hallway. She inserted the key into the lock and pushed the door open. "Welcome to the Washington Honeymoon Suite," she said, holding her arms out in a grand gesture.

"Oh hell," Grant mumbled under his breath.

Chapter 8

Turning my head, I took in the room. *Our* room. For a honeymoon suite, it definitely lived up to its name. Maggie got a fire started in the massive fireplace that was across from a king-sized sleigh bed, which would have dominated the space if not for how large the room was. Floor-to-ceiling bookcases covered the walls on either side of the fireplace. As beautiful as the room was, my eyes only seemed to be able to focus on the one bed.

"You folks were actually pretty lucky. This storm made it impossible for the newlyweds who paid for this room to make it. They decided to fly to Bermuda instead, but that means all the amenities they bought are now yours," Maggie said, pointing to a bottle of champagne that was chilling by the fireplace next to a platter of decadent chocolate-covered strawberries. I would have laughed if the whole situation didn't seem so ridiculous. How did I go from flying home for the holidays to being laid up in a honeymoon suite with my high school crush?

"This is fantastic," Grant said in a strangled voice, depositing me on the bed and backing up toward the door. "I better go see if the doctor is here," he said before fleeing from the room.

Maggie looked at me questioningly as I burst out laughing. "He's a bit of a commitment-phobe," I said, though it really wasn't funny. I had officially lost it.

"How long have you two been dating?" Maggie asked, taking my jacket and hanging it in the closet.

"Oh, no, we're not dating," I said, leaning back against the stack of pillows that lined the headboard. "We went to school together. It just so happens we ran into each other on our way home for the holidays. The funny thing is the trip has turned into something right out of the movies."

"That sounds like an interesting story."

"You could put it that way, but it's almost more appropriate to call it a disaster story," I admitted, launching into an explanation of everything that had happened in the last twenty-four hours. Maggie found the retelling of our adventure extremely humorous. We were both laughing when Grant returned with the doctor.

"Hello, young lady, I'm Doc Jones," the elderly gentleman said, holding out his hand. "I heard you hurt your ankle playing in the snow," he added, winking at me.

"That's one way to put it," I answered as Maggie giggled again. I grinned back, which turned into a laugh when Grant looked at both of us like we had sprouted an extra head. Doc Jones paid no attention as he moved to the foot of the bed where my sore ankle was propped up over a stack of pillows.

"The first thing I'm going to do is remove your boot, which will cause some discomfort," he said, tugging on my boot. Discomfort was a total understatement. I wanted to yell the whole dictionary of curse words, but I didn't want to shock everyone in the room. I leaned back against the pillows, panting as the doc examined my foot. I tried to appear tough for my audience, but all I really wanted to do was cry. My ankle, which had been merely throbbing, now felt like someone had taken a sledgehammer to it. Only when I heard Maggie clucking her tongue sympathetically did I raise my head off the pillows so I could peer at my right ankle. I studied it critically, not believing it was mine. It was easily twice its normal size, if not bigger. The most startling aspect was the color. The normal creamy tone of my skin was gone and replaced by an icky rainbow of blues, blacks and purples that all blended together into a bright swollen mess.

    I sank back against the pillow again as Doc Jones continued to probe at the monstrosity that was now my ankle. I knew he was being gentle as he could, but it felt like he was running it through a meat grinder. I turned my head from the others as a tear crept out of the corner of my eye. I wanted to tell him he was examining a swollen ankle, not working in a pottery class.

    "Well, I'm ninety-nine percent sure it's just a really bad sprain, but I'm going to wrap it good until we can get X-rays done to make sure. The closest hospital is twenty miles away, but we should wait until the storm has passed," he said, pulling a bandage from his bag. By the time he was done, a thin layer of sweat had beaded up on my forehead, but the pain was at least bearable now that the ankle was wrapped.

    Finally, when my foot was propped up again, I looked over at Grant, who had remained stoically silent during the examination.

    "Maggie, dear, will you get Jamie something to drink for her pain pills?" Doc Jones asked, pulling out a sample pack of pills. "These will help with the pain and might make you a little loopy, so no alcohol," he said, looking pointedly at the champagne.

"Can't I just take ibuprofen?" I asked, not liking the idea of taking pain pills with Grant around. Especially if they were supposed to make me loopy.

"Ibuprofen should work tomorrow, but for tonight you're going to want to take these," he said, popping two of the pills out of the pack.

Maggie handed me the glass of ice water she had poured from the ceramic pitcher on the highboy dresser. She winked at me as Doc handed over the pills. She knew why I didn't want to take them.

I stuck my tongue out at her before dropping the pills into my mouth. She laughed as she headed for the door. "I better go check on supper. Are you up to joining us in the dining room, or would you like me to bring a tray up?" she asked me.

"I'd like to join you if that's okay," I said, looking at the doctor questioningly.

"As long as you keep your foot propped up, that will be fine," he said, closing his bag.

"Would you like to join us, Doc?" Maggie asked. "I made pot roast," she added, trying to entice him.

"Damn, I sure hate passing up your pot roast, but June and Tim already invited me over for dinner.

You know it's dang near impossible for me to turn down June's chicken pot pie," he said, smiling at Grant and me. "You take it easy, young lady. I'll come back tomorrow evening to check your ankle," he said, heading for the door.

"Wait, what do I owe you?" I asked.

"Think nothing of it. Maybe one day you'll pass through again and take me out for a fancy dinner," he said, winking at me before leaving the room.

"I can't believe how nice everyone has been," I said, completely perplexed.

Grant laughed. "I know, right? But you know what? I'd like to think anyone in Woodfalls would do the same thing if two strangers like us needed a hand. Maybe when we get home we can think of some way to pay them back."

"That can't happen soon enough, let me tell you. Tomorrow we're calling the rental company and figuring out a way to get us another car so we can get home.

"You know we're going to have to wait until the storm passes, right?" Grant said, snagging two of the strawberries off the tray. He handed me one before popping the other in his mouth.

I gaped at him for a moment, ignoring the strawberry.

"What?" he asked at my guppy-like expression.

"We're not leaving tomorrow?"

"Jams, have you missed the blizzard outside? We're not going anywhere until it passes and they clear the roads. Tim was saying it could be Friday."

"But, Christmas is on Thursday—in three days," I said, stating the obvious. There was no way I could spend the next three days holed up in some honeymoon suite with him. "What am I going to do about my mom?" I added.

He sat on the edge of the bed beside me, which momentarily distracted me. Did he have to be so freaking handsome?

He smiled at me. Oh hell, did I say that out loud? It was the damn pills. I could already feel their effect as my brain took on a hazy quality.

"My mom wanted me home for Christmas," I said lamely, trying to cover up what I may or may not have said.

"Jams, I've known your family my whole life and I'm pretty sure your parents would rather you were safe. Plus, you heard Doc Jones. You need to keep your foot elevated."

His words made sense, or at least I thought they did. Just to be safe, I nodded my head. Again, I think I nodded my head. I was finding it hard to concentrate on what we were even talking about. Whatever had been in the pills had broken my brain, but at least I could no longer feel the pain in my ankle.

"Jamie, are you okay?" Grant asked, looking at me with concern.

"I'm okie dokie artichokie," I sang, giggling at my rhyme.

"I'm taking that to mean your pain pills are working," he said, moving around to the other side of the bed.

"Just put it this way. I feeeeeeeeel good," I slurred.

"I bet you do," he laughed, lying back against the pillows. For some reason, his action struck me as funny.

"I've always wanted you in the sack," I blurted out. I sensed that I shouldn't have said that, but my tongue and brain seemed to be working against each other.

"You have, huh?" Grant said, turning on his side. "Do tell."

I tried to focus on his face, but that had become fuzzy too. "Yep, since high school," I answered, closing my eyes. "Because I loooooved you," I sang, smiling at how the words chimed through my head.

Grant said something else, but it took too much effort to decipher. And that was the last thing I remembered.

Chapter 9

My eyes fluttered open to the sounds of the wind howling outside and the fire crackling in the fireplace. I felt warm and cozy snuggled up in the bed with a large hand resting on my bare stomach where my shirt had ridden up. My groggy mind didn't connect the dots until I lifted my arms, spotting both my hands. Glancing down, I could see Grant's fingers splayed across my abdomen. Suddenly, hazy memories of last night began flooding my mind. I remembered Grant lying next to me on the bed and me saying something about how I wanted to get him in the sack. Oh God, it was the pills Doc Jones had given me. Were they pain pills or truth serum? I was pretty sure I told Grant I loved him too. I would have given anything for it to have been a bad dream, but the memories were too clear now. Grant was sleeping on his side, facing me, holding me securely against his body. I was tempted to stay there, basking in his embrace, but my mouth felt fuzzy from falling asleep without brushing my teeth. I shifted my body to climb off the bed, but when my foot touched the floor, my sprained ankle reminded me I wasn't ready to walk on my own.

I crumpled to the floor, crying out in pain. The bed creaked and Grant's head peeked over the side, seeing me sprawled out on the hardwood floor. Glancing at the clock on the mantle, I saw it was barely five a.m.

"What were you thinking?" Grant asked, appearing at my side. He kneeled down to help me stand.

"I forgot," I answered, feeling like a complete ass. "I'm sorry I woke you," I apologized, looking at him. He was shirtless like the night at the roach motel. My already fuzzy mouth became as dry as the desert as I took in his taut muscles and defined six-pack abs. He had the physique of someone who was no stranger to physical labor. My fingers wanted to reach out and trace the contour of his pecks that because of his height were at my eye level. They became even closer when he scooped me into his arms.

"Were you trying to get to the bathroom?" he asked. I heard his words, but they didn't quite register. My mind continued to be preoccupied with the fact that I was in his arms while he was practically naked. I ran my hand over his chest. His skin was as warm as I imagined it would be. My eyes found his as I continued to explore the planes of his muscular upper body. He didn't speak, but shifted his stance. I suddenly felt the stirrings of humiliation. Of course he felt uncomfortable. He had no interest in me. I pulled away from his body, but he tightened his hold on me. My breathing began to match my rapid pulse as his eyes focused on my lips. I was ready and hesitant at the same time. I wanted to feel those lips pressed against mine, but what would it mean for us?

"Bathroom?" he asked huskily, returning his stare to my eyes.

"Huh?" I answered. His words shook me back to reality and my pressing needs. Crap, my teeth. He almost kissed me and I'm sure my breath was rank enough to turn Medusa to stone. I clamped my hand over my mouth.

"Is that some kind of hint?" he asked in a strangled voice

"I need to brush my teeth," I mumbled around my fingers.

"Are you still high on those pills?" he asked, waiting like I was going to spout out more gibberish like I did last night.

I groaned at his words. "No, I just hate morning breath," I said, flushing. I vainly hoped the dim light from the fire would keep him from seeing my embarrassment. "Please stop looking at me like I just climbed out from under some gross rock," I begged, hoping he would just let the whole pill thing go. Couldn't it be like going to Vegas? What happens when Jamie takes pills stays at blah blah blah.

He stared at me for a moment before coming to the conclusion that I wasn't high. I was getting close to the point of becoming defensive by the way he was looking at me, but something in his stare struck a chord in me. It was almost as if he cared, which confused me, but still fueled my feelings of desire for him. The desire that had been dormant for the past five years since we'd last seen each other was now smoldering.

We continued to stare, both nervously waiting to see who would make the first move. I felt something akin to pain with need. I strained closer, willing him silently to ease the burning inside me. A log in the fireplace settled loudly, startling us both. The moment was broken like coming to from a hypnotic trance.

What was I doing here? Talk about playing with fire. Everything in me knew I was asking to get burned. It was time to get a grip. "Um, bathroom," I reminded him, seeking to get a little distance between us. As nice as it was to languish in his arms while I admired his physique, it was hard to want to go any further without wondering if I would only get hurt in the long run.

"Right," he said, heading for the bathroom. It didn't surprise me to see how luxurious the bathroom was in our suite. Admittedly, I was a definite bathroom slut and this one didn't disappoint. A large granite counter with grey smoke-colored glass bowl double sinks lined one wall. The best feature was the old-fashioned claw-footed tub that begged for long bubble baths, especially for two, judging by the size. This whole suite was like an aphrodisiac.

Grant placed me on the counter between the sinks, pulling my eyes from the tub where I was picturing us naked together. I was acting like a walking sex-deprived disaster. If I didn't come to grips with my feelings I would drive myself nuts. "I'll get your bathroom stuff," Grant said, seemingly oblivious to my erotic thoughts.

"Can you manage okay, or do you need my help?" he asked, returning quickly. He looked comfortable with either answer.

"I got it," I gulped. Even if I did think sharing a hot bubble bath together was a possibility, I couldn't imagine the best way to get us in the mood would be for him to help me use the potty.

"Just be careful. With your luck these last few days, it wouldn't be a far stretch for you to fall and really break something this time."

"Bite your tongue," I muttered, even though it was hard to deny his observation. Never in my whole life had I ever had such a string of bad luck. Maybe it wasn't me. He could be the bad luck charm for all we knew.

He laughed at my words and closed the door to give me my privacy. It took a lot of hobbling on one leg, but I was finally able to brush my teeth, wash my face, use the toilet and fix my hair so it no longer resembled a bird's nest. By the time I finished, I almost felt like I had completed a workout. I was ready to cut off my foot so I wouldn't have to deal with the pain.

Grant was standing patiently outside the bathroom when I opened the door. I was both disappointed and relieved to see that he had put on clothes. He had also opened the heavy drapes that I didn't realize covered a long bay window with a built-in window seat. The sky was still covered in clouds, but I could tell the sun was beginning to rise. Of course, it was still snowing. Grant carried me back to the bed, which he had made while I was in this bathroom. It was seriously too bad he had commitment issues, because he would make someone an amazing husband someday.

"Are you hungry?"

My stomach growled in response to his question, making him smile. "I'll take that as a yes. You should be hungry since you snored through dinner."

"I don't snore," I retorted.

"Are you sure about that?"

"No one's ever mentioned it before," my voice trailed off. Did I snore? It had been a long time since I had an overnight guest.

"Probably because I made it up," he said grinning at me as he headed for the door. Grabbing a pillow off the bed, I chucked it at the door, even though he was already long gone. He would never outgrow teasing me.

    I switched on the lamp on the table and picked up my phone that Grant must have charged for me since my battery was at one hundred percent. It was still too early to call my parents, but I would have to in a little while. I didn't relish breaking the news to my mom that for the first time ever, I would not be home for Christmas. Scrolling through my social media apps, I made sure I hadn't missed anything in my absence. For the most part, everything was quiet on that front. I guess everyone was in holiday mode, which was fine with me. It was kind of nice to take a break from it all.

    Setting my phone to the side, I laid back on the pillows. It felt strange to not be obsessing over my blog. For two years, I had slept, ate and breathed nothing but my cooking show. Even when I agreed to come home, my plan was to work while I was there. I had an entire Christmas segment worked out with different holiday treats that were sure to woo your man. Now, it almost felt like my perspective was changing, or was at least blurred. Maybe it was the nearly life-altering plane crash or the car accident during a snowstorm that could have turned tragic, or my sprained ankle. Or for that matter, even the night in the roach motel. I could laugh now at how crazy the last forty-eight hours had been, but it also had me thinking about where my life was going. Of course, I neglected to add the most important thing to the list, which was Grant. Up until two days ago, I had been able to successfully make it through long stretches of time without giving him any thought. Even if he did come to mind, it was only the fact that he was probably married to Amanda with a couple of kids. Knowing that wasn't the case changed everything.

"Sorry it took so long. Maggie insisted on making you a full breakfast," Grant said, interrupting my thoughts. He carried a tray loaded with food.

"Holy gluttony. She didn't have to do that," I protested, although the tantalizing scents had my growling stomach thinking otherwise.

"I tried to tell her that, but I think she felt bad since you missed dinner last night. Which, by the way, might have been the best pot roast I've ever had," he said, placing the tray in the middle of the bed between us. He handed one of the loaded plates to me.

"So, tell me what's been going on in Woodfalls," I said, taking a bite of bacon.

"Doesn't your mom keep you up on everything?"

"Not really. Sometimes I think she's hoping that by being close-mouthed I'll come home more often. She'll throw out little teasers every once in a while, but won't embellish on them, even when I press her. She's a jerk," I said affectionately.

"Sounds smart to me. What do you want to know?"

"Everything," I answered.

And that's what he did. He filled me in on who was dating who, who had recently had kids, who had passed away, and of course, my cousin Tressa's latest scandals. I loved Tressa to death, but I swear, she wasn't happy unless she was stirring up something. Our conversation continued after we finished eating. He was turning into an easy person to talk to when he wasn't teasing me. I'm sure a lot of it had to do with our common bond of knowing all the same people. I was surprised to discover we shared a lot of the same likes and dislikes. It seemed crazy that even growing up around someone in the same small town didn't mean you knew everything about them.

"What about your dad? How's he liking retirement?" I asked, sliding my plate away so I would stop nibbling on the leftovers. My stomach was threatening mutiny if I tried to eat one more morsel of food.

"Well, considering he still comes in almost every day, I'd hardly call it retirement. I think he missed the memo on what retirement is supposed to entail. I guess I can't blame him though. The lumber yard has been his whole life since he was kid. My grandpa was the same way. I'm sure when it's my turn it'll be my son griping one day."

"Your son? You want kids?" I asked, completely floored.

"Sure I want kids. The more, the better as far as I'm concerned."

Seriously? Mr. Non-Commit wanted kids? Did he understand that kids were the mother of all commitments?

"What? You don't want kids?" he asked intently.

"Of course I want kids. I want a whole houseful, but I'm shocked you want them."

"Why? You think I'd make a lousy dad?" he asked, snagging the last piece of bacon from my plate.

"Of course not, but you do realize you'll actually have to bite the bullet and commit to someone?"

"Duh, really?" he said, looking offended.

"Hey, don't get all offended. You're the one who said you couldn't commit."

"What? When did I say something like that?" he asked incredulously.

"When you were talking about Amanda getting married," I answered, amazed at how dense he was being.

"I said she wanted things from me I wasn't willing to give."

"Exactly. Considering she got married to someone else, I'm guessing what she wanted was marriage."

"Right," he answered, looking at me like I was the one talking in circles and not him.

"Which would mean you were unable to commit," I said through gritted teeth, plopping back on my pillows. He was so infuriating at times. I couldn't tell if he was messing with me.

"Commit to *her* being the point."

"Ooooh, you didn't want to marry her," I said, finally understanding. I pulled my bottom lip into my mouth, mulling his words over. He wasn't the commitment-phobe I had portrayed him to be. He just hadn't found his "someone." I couldn't help the smile that spread across my face. It shouldn't matter to me. But it did.

"Ding ding ding. I don't remember you being that dense in school. Have these highlights messed with your brain?" he teased, tugging on a lock of my hair.

"Funny. I thought you were deliberately trying to be obtuse."

"Why do you care so much?" he asked, scooting the tray to the foot of the bed and moving closer to me.

My body reacted to his close proximity. "What makes you think I care?" I said breathlessly as he inched closer.

"I think you care a lot," he said, dropping his eyes to my mouth.

I swallowed hard as his mouth hovered close to mine. "Tell me you haven't been thinking about this," he said, stroking a thumb over my bottom lip.

"Have you?" I whispered.

"Jams, I've been thinking about this longer than I can remember," he said, crushing his lips to mine. His words rang through my head, but there was no way I could make sense of them when his lips felt so good. I responded with a small moan when his tongue trailed across the same spot where his thumb had been. My pleasure filled acceptance affected him and he dragged me into his arms, deepening the kiss. A shiver rippled down my body as our tongues found each other. I gripped the hem of his shirt, wanting him closer. Hearing my unspoken plea, he settled the upper half of his body on top of mine. I gasped with pleasure, running my fingers up under his shirt. I could feel the firmness of his muscles and smoothness of his skin. It was almost my undoing when I felt him tugging at my shirt moments before his hand glided over the sensitive skin of my ribcage. My blood roared through me. His hand moved farther up to my breasts and I bowed my body, whimpering against his lips. I wanted his touch everywhere on my body.

"Jams, you're seriously killing me," he said raggedly against my lips. He pulled back slightly.

"Is that good or bad?" I asked, running my hands up his torso. My fingers trailed to the small patch of hair that disappeared down his jeans. Ever since I'd seen him in nothing but his jockey shorts the other night, I've fantasized about that small trail of hair.

"So good it almost hurts," he said, leaning in for another kiss. Before his lips could reach their destination, a beeping noise from downstairs followed by the sound of voices in the hallway interrupted us. "Really?" he asked incredulously, climbing off the bed. I couldn't help giggling. Of course something was going on. With our luck lately, I could have almost set my watch by it.

Chapter 10

Grant helped me put my boot on my one good foot and slid his feet into his own before he reached for me. His eyes were amused as he scooped me up into his arms yet again. "Nice timing," he joked. "I better think about baseball and hope it works quickly."

"What?" I asked, not getting what he meant.

"You know—we were just doing some stuff that may have caused something," he said, nodding his head downward.

I burst out laughing after finally realizing his problem. "So, I shouldn't tell you how hot you were making me?" I said, adding fuel to the fire.

"Please no," he pleaded as I reached out to open the door.

In the last twenty-four hours, I had been held by him a number of times, and yet this time it felt different as he cradled me tenderly against his chest. We followed another couple down the stairs and outside. Smoke was drifting from the back of the house, which alarmed us both.

"Where's Maggie?" I asked, scanning the small crowd outside.

"I don't know," Grant said, looking worriedly back inside.

"Put me down, I can hang on to the post," I said, hearing sirens in the background.

"Don't move," he said, setting me down.

"I promise not to run any marathons. Now get in there."

A woman I didn't know came over to stand beside me. "Are you okay?" she asked as I hobbled on one foot while I held the banister.

"Yeah, it's just a bad sprain. Do you know what happened?" I asked.

"I think it's another one of Maggie's mishaps in the kitchen," she laughed.

"This has happened before?" I asked, feeling somewhat relieved.

"Oh, yeah. We've been coming here for ten years, and I think Maggie has had a fire five of those years," she said, laughing again. "I was still snoozing when the alarm went off this time. Thank god my husband, Jim, heard it since I sleep like the dead. I wish he would have had the foresight to tell me to grab my shoes though," she said, pointed down to her stocking-clad feet.

I nodded my head absentmindedly. The sirens were getting louder, but I was more concerned that it seemed to be taking Grant so long. The rest of the residents didn't seem overly concerned as they chatted among themselves, but I was still a worried. Just when I was ready to hobble in after him, the first fire truck turned down the narrow lane in front of the inn. At the same moment, Grant came out from the house followed by a sheepish-looking Maggie, who was coughing from the smoke.

"Not again, Maggie," one of the firemen said, climbing down from the rig. "Is it out?"

"It was just a small one, Hank," Maggie said, shooting a guilty look at her guests.

"What did we tell you about using your gas stove?" he asked as the other men from the fire truck headed inside to make sure the fire was indeed out. Peering through the door, I could tell most of the smoke had already started to thin out.

"What happened?" I asked Grant as Maggie trailed in after the firemen.

"Grease fire. Maggie had it out by the time I made it in there, but the kitchen was already filled with smoke. We opened the back door and the kitchen windows to let it blow out," he said, taking my hand so I wasn't so wobbly. "I guess it's happened before. Maggie likes to keep the bacon grease on the stove, but she forgets to turn off the heat under it."

I laughed. I had worked long enough in the cooking field to know her mistake.

"Well, at least Maggie seems to be a pro at dealing with it," I said, watching the firemen head back out. Hank was still reprimanding Maggie, telling her he'd have to give her a citation the next time they had to come out. Maggie listened to him solemnly, nodding her head in all the appropriate spots. Once the fire truck pulled away, Maggie turned to me with the same mischievous grin I had seen the day before.

"Sorry about the early morning wake-up call, folks. The good news is breakfast is ready for those who haven't eaten and the cookies in the oven were saved before disaster struck," she said good-naturedly, leading the way back into the house. Everyone laughed with her, relieved it was nothing more serious. That, and we really wanted to get back inside. There were far too many chattering teeth as everyone stomped their feet in the cold. At least the snow had finally stopped, but the wind was still blowing around.

"Your chariot waits," Grant said, lifting me up. "I think I'm getting used to this."

"Fine by me," I teased. My eyes met his and I knew we were both thinking about our kiss and everything else that was about to happen before the ruckus. His eyes darkened while his grip on me tightened. "You want to go back upstairs?" he asked. I knew what he was asking. If we went upstairs, we would be continuing where we left off. He was giving me a chance to put on the brakes, but it wasn't necessary. I was as ready as he was.

I nodded my head, running my hand over the light-colored five o'clock shadow covering the lower half of his face. I liked this rugged look he was sporting. I continued to explore his face, taking time to trace my finger over his lip as he carried me back to our room. He startled me by sucking the finger into his mouth. My stomach tightened with desire as his tongue swirled sensually around my finger. I turned my head to see how close we were to our room. Sensing my urgency, he picked up his pace.

Our door was still open from when we left earlier, but Grant kicked it closed behind us and reached back to make sure it was locked. "I don't want to hurt your ankle," he said, looking at my wrapped foot.

"You won't," I said. At the moment, that was the last thing on my mind. My desire for him had intensified to the point of no return. I had dreamed about this moment for a long time. As he lowered me to the bed, I remembered something I wanted to ask him. "What did you mean when you said you'd been thinking about kissing me for a long time?" I asked as he pulled off my boot and climbed up on the bed with me. Taking care not to jar my ankle, he positioned me on my side so we were facing each other.

He scooted close, running a hand from my shoulder down to my hand before lacing our fingers together. He brought my hand to his mouth so he could place his lips on my knuckles before answering me. "Jams, surely you know I've had a thing for you half my life?" he said, placing a hot kiss on my wrist.

"No, you haven't," I argued. Did I really need to remind him of all the relentless teasing he had put me through during my formative years?

"Didn't you get the hint when I dipped your braid in paint in second grade?" he asked, scooting my shirtsleeve up so he could trail his lips up my forearm. I shifted closer to him with my desire at full force. Sensing my needs, he lifted my good leg and eased his own leg between me, bringing us practically on top of each other. I couldn't help moving against him. He was driving me nuts with his slow patient pace.

"You hated me," I said, finally finding my voice since our slow grinding motion was distracting me.

"I was just trying to get your attention. I thought you were cute, but you kept shooting me down," he said, moving his kisses from my arm to my collarbone.

"You teased me mercifully."

"I had a major hound dog crush on you. I worked for a week on the valentine I gave you in third grade. Do you remember it?"

"I still have it," I admitted.

He pulled back from my neck for a moment. "You do?" he asked, sounding thunderstruck.

I nodded my head as his eyes held mine. "I had to re-tape it freshman year when I tore it up."

"Why, what happened freshman year?" he asked, smoothing my hair off my forehead before resting his hand on my thigh so he could hitch my leg over his more securely. We continued our slow grind. I would have been embarrassed, but it felt too good to care.

"You started dating Amanda. It crushed my heart, so I tore up the heart you gave me. After I re-retaped it, I shoved it in my drawer so I wouldn't have to face it."

"I started dating Amanda because I thought you were never going to give me a shot. The guys were giving me a hard time and told me to do something or move on. I figured they were right when you never looked at me again."

"You broke my heart. Just ask Fran. She was my sounding board the entire time," I whispered as he lowered his mouth to my cheek.

"I was stupid. If it makes you feel better, you broke my heart too when you left Woodfalls," he admitted.

My heart stuttered. His words eclipsed our sensual heat as we shared probably the most significant moment of my life. "We were both stupid," I said, pulling him close. I couldn't stand another moment without our lips together. The kiss started so tenderly that tears formed in my eyes. Cupping my face with his hands, Grant anchored me in place as his lips staked their claim. I deepened the kiss and moved my hips to force his leg more snugly between mine. His hands found their way under my shirt, moving seductively over my stomach, past my ribcage and coming to a rest right below my bra line. "Yes," I whimpered. I raised my back to allow him access to remove my lacy undergarment.

"You want this?" he asked, slowly lifting my bra so his hand could make its way underneath.

"Don't be a tease," I said, tugging on his shirt.

"But you're so cute when you get aggravated," he said, shrugging off his shirt. I lifted my head and circled his nipple with my tongue, grinning wickedly when his eyes darkened. I could play his game if that's what he wanted. I glided my tongue smoothly to his other nipple, dragging it between my teeth and biting gently. His body arched against mine. I could feel his hunger pressed hot and hard against me. Enjoying the feeling of empowerment, I sucked harder on his chest as he gripped my hair in his hands.

"Enough, woman," he finally said, pulling off my shirt and bra.

"Just thought you needed a little taste of your own medicine," I said. He took it as a challenge and began kissing my stomach. This time it was my turn to arch as his mouth left a fiery path down my abdomen to the top of my PJ bottoms. To make his point, he lifted the edge of my panties and placed one more purposeful kiss just above where I wanted him the most. He was killing me. My response set a fast course as we shed the rest of our clothing. I finally got to see where the enticing trail of hair on his stomach ended just before he settled between my legs. His eyes never left mine as he moved slowly inside me. He set the pace, which was both infuriating and toe curling all at once. He would thrust against me, getting me right to the edge and then hold back to drag the moment out. I clutched at his back, urging him that I was close.

"Not yet, baby. I want this to last. We've waited a long time for it," he said, placing his mouth tenderly on mine. I moved restlessly beneath him, completely consumed by the fire. Just when I thought I couldn't handle it a second longer, he started moving inside me again. The wave came out of nowhere, crushing me as I pressed my hips against him. His lips swallowed my moans of pleasure as my body convulsed around his. He finished just as I did, thrusting one last time before collapsing on top of me.

Completely content, I stroked a hand over his head, marveling at how good his weight felt on top of me. My eyes felt heavy and I could feel his labored breathing returning to normal. I think we both must have dozed for a few minutes, but eventually Grant left the bed to clean up before closing the drapes. He crawled back in bed and gathered me in his arms. We napped into the early afternoon together.

Chapter 11

The echo of laughter in the hallway woke me a few hours later. Turning to face Grant, I saw he was already awake and watching me.

"What?" I asked, self-consciously pulling the blanket up to cover my breasts.

"I'm just basking in the glory of finally having you in my bed," he said, tightening his arm that was wrapped around my midriff.

"Well, technically, I was in your bed last night too," I teased. "Oh crap, I keep forgetting to call my mom. She's going to kill me," I said, sitting up in a sudden panic.

"Relax. I called her last night while you were whacked out on your happy pills," Grant said, placing his hand on mine before I could dial my parents' house.

"You did?" I asked, touched that he had the foresight to do that. "Wait, what did you tell her?"

"I told her about the snowstorm and our accident," he said, chuckling as he ticked off everything that had happened in the last day. "Oh, and your ankle. She said with the luck we're having, her advice was to stay put, but of course, that was before the fire here this morning too," he added as we both started laughing at the hilarity of the situation. We regained our composure and Grant got up to start a bubble bath in the big claw-footed tub. Trying to take a bath with him while also trying not to get my bandaged ankle wet was quite a feat. Still, our two slippery bodies combined with his roving hands made it the best bath I had ever taken. We didn't make it back to the bed before he took me again on the bathroom counter.

Once we got cleaned up, I finally called my parents to make sure they were really okay with me missing Christmas with them. My mom reassured me it was perfectly fine. At first I was confused about her complete one eighty until I pieced together she was tickled pink that I was cooped up with Grant. I'm sure she wanted nothing more than for Grant and me to have a real relationship. I knew her too well and in her mind she saw it as a way to get me back to Woodfalls on a permanent basis. I hung up the phone, reassuring her I would call again tomorrow and then again on Christmas Day.

Grant and I finally made an appearance downstairs in the late afternoon when Doc Jones came by to check on my ankle. It was still horrifically swollen and more discolored than the day before, but I turned down more of his happy pills, settling for ibuprofen instead. He stuck around for dinner, which was steaming bowls of stew and homemade bread followed by cherry cobbler. During dinner, I learned the three other couples knew each other. They were older than we were and had no family to speak of, so they spent the holidays at Maggie's Bed and Breakfast every year.

"It's because her cooking is out of this world," one of the husbands said, winking at Maggie, who blushed.

"Even if I do set a few fires," Maggie joked, clearing the table. The rest of us laughed as we headed out to the living room with the coffee Maggie had prepared.

Doc Jones excused himself after one cup. "I'll come check on you again tomorrow."

"You don't have to. It's Christmas Eve," I protested.

"Darling, why do you think I'll be coming by? I'm hoping Maggie will invite me over for Christmas Eve dinner," he said, winking at me as Maggie came in drying her hands on her apron.

"Oh, posh. You know you're always invited. Aunt June and Uncle Tim wouldn't have it any other way," Maggie said, walking him to the door.

After Doc left, the rest of us sat around chatting well into the night. The other couples were all hilarious as they regaled us with their own mishaps over the years. Grant kept an arm around me the entire evening, like he was afraid I would disappear if he didn't hold me. I didn't mind at all, especially since his fingers played with the hairs at the back of my neck the entire time. Maggie noticed our closeness and gave me a wink when no one was looking. I returned her grin enjoying the moment.

Retiring for the evening, Grant and I made love for the third time on the plush carpet in front of the fireplace in our room. Unlike the previous two times, this was more of a sensual dance as we used our hands and mouths to explore each other's bodies and discover our hidden pleasures.

The next morning the sun was shining brightly for the first time in three days. I bathed solo in the tub as Grant washed my hair while I worried about keeping my bandaged foot dry. Once we were dressed, he carried me downstairs and deposited me in the living room, claiming there were a few things he needed to do. Perplexed but also intrigued, I let him have his secrets while I helped Maggie prepare some of the food for the evening. We had learned the night before that Maggie hosted a Christmas Eve party for friends and family members before they all headed off to midnight mass. She put out a buffet spread that everyone else contributed dishes to as well.

    Maggie turned on Christmas carols while we worked. Even though I wasn't home in Woodfalls, it still helped make it feel special. I even found myself humming along. It was funny to think that like a Scrooge, I had fought my mom tooth and nail about coming home for Christmas. I had my reasons, but none of them seemed to matter as much anymore. That was the irony of Christmas this year. Now that I really wanted to be home, I couldn't get there. Sitting in Maggie's kitchen preparing cake pops and decorating Christmas cookies, I was reminded of the true importance of Christmas. It was all about spending time with loved ones. The essence of

Christmas was happiness and togetherness. I would never forget that again.

Grant returned to the house a few hours later with a silly grin plastered to his face. He wouldn't tell me what he was up to. "You have to wait," he said, smiling the entire time. I grumbled my displeasure, but it was an act. The guests began to arrive before I could quiz him any further. I was pleased to see June again, who greeted me like an old friend. She clucked sympathetically over my foot, though she pointed out if we would have listened to her in the first place, it wouldn't have happened. I had to agree with her, although having a bum ankle definitely had its perks, like being held in Grant's arms.

I lost track of Grant as more and more people came and went. Maggie and June introduced me to everyone, which was a bit overwhelming. After a while, I stopped trying to remember their names. I was in the middle of discussing my food blog with Maggie and her friends when Grant found me.

"Are you ready for your surprise?" he whispered in my ear.

"Yes," I shivered as his breath tickled my ear.

"I'll bring her back in a few minutes," he told Maggie and her friends, scooping me up in his arms.

They all sighed collectively. We paused in the hallway and he set me down to help me into my jacket before carrying me out the front door. I'm not sure what I had been expecting when he told me he had a surprise, but he managed to shock me.

Parked in front of the inn was a gorgeous Clydesdale horse attached to a beautiful carriage. Tim sat at the reigns, giving me a small wave.

"Your carriage awaits my lady," Grant said, placing me in the seat before joining me on the other side. He tucked a couple blankets around our laps as Tim urged the horse to move.

"How did you know?" I asked.

"Know what?" he asked, placing an arm around my shoulder.

"This has always been my Christmas dream."

"I knew that, Jams. Haven't you been paying attention? I remember everything, including in fourth grade when Ms. McMillan had us all write our Christmas wishes on the board. Your wish that year was to ride on a horse-drawn carriage on Christmas," he said.

Tears welled up in my eyes. "You made my Christmas wish come true," I said, enchanted as I looked up at him. Who would have thought? Grant—

the boy who had teased me and driven me insane—remembered something I had wished for almost fifteen years ago. A tear escaped my overflowing eyes. Grant caught it with his thumb.

"Jams, I want to make all your wishes come true. Merry Christmas," he said, capturing my mouth with his.

I didn't tell him he already had.

Enjoy the first two chapters from

Misunderstandings
A Woodfalls Girls novel
By Tiffany King

Available May 6, 2014 from the Berkley Publishing Group.

Penguin (USA) Inc.

Just when she thought things were going up...

Two years after a devastating breakup, Brittni Mitchell has moved on from Justin Avery—or so she tells herself. But when she returns to Seattle for her best friend's engagement party, Brittni finds herself the victim of a disastrously timed elevator breakdown. She's trapped with the last person she wants to face, and forced to recount the past she desperately wants to forget.

She's going to have to look back...

When Brittni left her podunk hometown for a big city college experience at the University of Washington, hooking up with a guy like Justin Avery was not part of her plan. Between Justin's attention-grabbing tattoos, cigarette smoking, and bad boy attitude Brittni quickly chalked him up as "Mr. Wrong." But his charm was unrelenting, and Brittni's decision to give Justin a chance quickly turned into the worst choice she ever made.

So that she might be able to move forward.

Now she's stuck with Justin—literally—and the complicated web of misunderstandings that tied up the truth for two years is about to unravel.

"Super sweet and swoon-worthy!"— #1 *New York Times* Bestselling author Jennifer L. Armentrout

"Funny, real, moving and passionate, Misunderstandings is a MUST-READ for NA contemporary romance fans."--*New York Times* bestselling author Samantha Young

THE BERKLEY PUBLISHING GROUP
Published by the Penguin Group
Penguin Group (USA) Inc.

Copyright © 2013 by Tiffany King
License Notes
This ebook is licensed for your personal enjoyment only. This ebook may not be re-sold or given away to other people. If you would like to share this book with another person, please purchase an additional copy for each recipient. If you're reading this book and did not purchase it, or it was not purchased for your use only, then please purchase your own copy. Thank you for respecting the hard work of this author.
All rights reserved. Except as permitted under the U.S. Copyright Act of 1976, no part of this publication may be reproduced, distributed, or transmitted in any form or by any means, electronic, mechanical, photocopying, recording, or otherwise, or stored in a database or retrieval system, without the prior written permission of the publisher.
The characters and events portrayed in this book are fictitious. Any similarity to real persons, living or dead is coincidental and not intended by the author.

Chapter One

```
Present Day

11:02 am
```

    The rain was coming down in steady sheets as I stepped from the yellow taxi that had deposited me in front of Columbia Center in Seattle. "Keep the change," I said to the driver as I reached back inside the taxi to pay my fare. I stood momentarily with the rain pelting my face, tilting my head back to see the top of the tallest building in the state of Washington—all seventy-six floors of it. I knew that fact because I looked it up on the Internet. I needed to get an idea of what I would be dealing with. Not that my friend Rob, who I was here to see, worked on the top floor, but it was close. His office was on the fifty-second floor, which meant a long tortuous elevator ride. Something I wasn't looking forward to at all. Back home in Woodfalls, the tallest building was the three-story Wells Fargo bank they had built across from Smith's General Store a few years back. I was attending college at the University of Washington at the time, but back in Woodfalls it was big news. My mom, the town's resident busybody, made sure I received daily updates about the construction. Now, standing here, the building in front of me made our little bank back home look like a dollhouse.

The rain was beginning to find its way down the generic yellow raincoat I had purchased from the Seattle airport just that morning. The pilot had gleefully informed us before landing that Seattle was having its rainiest September in years. The irony that the rainiest state in the country was having its rainiest year in history was not lost on me. Why wouldn't it be cold, rainy and miserable? It matched the way I felt about this place. Of course, that wasn't always the case. When I first arrived in Seattle three years ago, I was a greenhorn from my Podunk hometown. That's why I had chosen UW. It was as far away from Woodfalls as I could possibly get without applying to the University of Hawaii. Three years ago, I had decided that nine months of rainy weather was a fair trade-off to finally be surrounded by civilization. That and it was hundreds of miles away from my often annoying but well-intentioned mother. The endless array of restaurants, museums, stores and the music scene had tantalized me, making me vividly realize just how lacking and uncultured Woodfalls was. Everything about Seattle intrigued me, making me never want to leave, but Puget Sound was by far my favorite thing about being there. On the weekends I would haul my laptop and textbooks down to one of the cafés on the waterfront. I would spend hours drinking coffee and working on schoolwork. That is, when people watching didn't distract me. That trait is something I had obviously inherited from my mom. Still, everything had been going along just the way I had imagined it would. It was liberating to be out from under my mom's thumb and the prying eyes of everyone back home. Here I could be my own person, with my own life. Then everything went to hell. I met Justin Avery—the whirlwind hurricane who left my head spinning and my stomach dropping to my knees like I was on a roller coaster.

My thoughts were broken when a wave of water splashed up from the road, soaking my pants from the knees down. "Terrific," I grumbled, looking down at the ruined pair of strappy sandals I had just bought. This is what I got for abandoning my typical attire of jeans and Converse shoes.

Stepping away from the offending curb before another rogue wave of nasty puddle water could finish the job, I focused on making it into the building without busting my ass, or worse yet, breaking my neck. The fake leather that had seemed so smooth and comfortable when I bought the sandals was now doing a great impersonation of a roller skate. My toes were also threatening mutiny from the cold, only adding insult to injury. This was the gagillionth reason why I had vowed never to return to Seattle. The city and I had bad blood between us.

The only reason I was standing here now was for Melissa and Rob, my two best friends from college who demanded that I be here for their engagement party. I tried every feasible excuse I could come up with—"I'm sick," "I'm out of the country," "I can't get off work." No excuse seemed to stand up to Melissa's bullshit meter.

"You're one of our best friends. You have to be here," Melissa insisted.

"No. I hate you. I'm not your friend. I never was your friend," I said.

"I wish you could see the world's smallest violin I'm playing for you right now. Come on. Pull on your big girl panties and stop hiding."

An uncomfortable silence interrupted the conversation before Melissa finally spoke up again. "I'm sorry, Brittni. I'm a bitch for even saying that. I just mean you can't let what happened dictate your life forever," Melissa had reasoned. "Besides, you're my maid of honor. I need you. Just think of this trip as a test, like dipping your toes in water. Chances are you'll hardly see him, and if you do, it's not like you guys even have to talk."

"Maybe," I said. "I'll talk to you later."

"You mean you'll see me lat—" Her words were cut off as I ended the call.

"Maybe" was the best answer I could give at the moment. The only hope I had left was my boss.

"It's a good time to go since I'll need you more next month," Ms. Miller, my principal at Woodfalls Elementary, had stated. "Mary Smith has her wrist surgery scheduled for October, and won't be able to return to work until February. I swear, I've never seen someone so damn gleeful over a surgery. I'm sure it has something to do with that godawful book-reader thingy she got for Christmas. She's always crowing about some new author she's discovered," Ms. Miller added, looking perplexed. "Me, I need an actual book in my hand, not some electronic doodad that will most likely come alive and kill me in my sleep."

"I'm thinking now might be a good time to lay off the science fiction flicks," I had countered dryly as I tried to squish the unease that had settled in the pit of my stomach. That was that. Ms. Miller was the only obstacle left. It seemed fate wanted me in Seattle.

Now, two weeks later, here I was with my shoes squishing across the tile floor of Columbia Center. It was glaringly obvious that nothing good could come from me returning to Seattle. I skirted around a security guard and headed for the women's bathroom so I could survey the damage.

"Holy shit," I muttered when I took in my appearance in the long expansion of mirrors that lined the wall. I looked like a drowned rat. My long hair that I had painstakingly straightened earlier had been replaced with my typical corkscrew curls that were the bane of my existence. "Damn," I sighed as I pulled my compact from my purse so I could repair my makeup-streaked face. This was just another sign I shouldn't be here. If my friend Rob wasn't expecting me for lunch, I would have chalked it up as a lost cause and headed back to my hotel. At the moment, I'd gladly trade my soaked clothing and frozen toes for solitude in my hotel room.

    "Get a grip, wimp-ass," I chastised myself out loud, ignoring a startled look from a form-fitting suit-clad woman before she hustled out of the bathroom. "Yeah, keep moving. Nothing to see here but the freako talking to herself in the bathroom," I said, grabbing a handful of paper towels to mop up my feet and legs. Tressa, my best friend back in Woodfalls, would have a field day if she saw what a mess I was; and Ashton, my other friend, would laugh and make a joke about it. I was supposed to be the one who never got frazzled and always held it together. Tressa was the more dramatic one of our trio. She made snap decisions often, never giving any thought to the consequences. Growing up, I was often left holding the short end of the stick in most of her escapades, but I didn't care. I envied her fearless attitude. I could have used an ounce of her fearlessness at the moment. I was the cautious one. The overanalyzer, skeptical, glass-is-half-empty kind of girl. Only once had I thrown caution to the wind, and it had bitten me in the ass. That one mistake was never far from my mind. How could it be? I left town and ran back home because of it. Being back in the scene of my troubles didn't help the situation. I needed to get my act together. Two years was a long time ago. I needed to buck up or whatever shit they say to get someone to stop freaking out.

I pulled my brush from my bag and ran it through my damp blonde locks, cringing as it tugged through the tangled curls that had taken over my head. After a futile moment of trying to make it look more dignified and less like a refuge for wayward birds, I gave up and threw it in a clip, which at least made it so that I no longer looked like the Bride of Frankenstein from those cheesy black-and-white movies. I added a layer of my favorite lipstick and finally felt halfway normal.

"You got this," I said, pivoting around and striding out of the bathroom. I ignored the eruption of laughter from the two giggling girls who were entering as I was leaving. Obviously, I would be their comedic relief for the day.

I straightened up, finding the backbone that had liquefied and all but disappeared the moment the plane's wheels had touched down on the wet tarmac that morning. "Screw him. He doesn't own the city. I have every right to be here," I told myself as I headed for the long bank of elevators to the right of the bathrooms. A small crowd of people hurried onto one of the elevators as the doors slid open. I declined to join the overflowing box, waiting instead for the next elevator that would be less crowded. Being closed in with a group of strangers wouldn't cut it for me. I couldn't stand being in confined spaces anyway, but elevators and I had a hate/hate kind of relationship. I hated them, and if the seventh grade hand crushing incident was any indication, they hated me too.

"No problem. The doors will open and you will step inside. Nice and easy," I whispered to myself. I knew it would require all my will and strength to remain sane on the elevator as it carried me up fifty-two floors to Rob's office. As is always the case with my luck, he couldn't have been on the first five or so floors, making the stairs a viable option. N-o-o-o-o-o, it had to be practically up in the clouds.

The ding signifying the arrival of the next car prompted me out of my inner whine-fest. I took a deep breath as if I were about to jump into water before cautiously stepping aboard the elevator. I exhaled a sigh of relief as the doors slowly closed and I found myself alone for the impending ride up. This was a good thing in case my hyperventilating-I-wish-I-sucked-my-thumb-or-at-least-had-a-stiff-drink elevator behavior decided to surface.

My relief was short-lived when a hand reached between the closing doors, causing them to reopen.

"You know, sticking your hand in like that can result in serious injury." Personal experience had me pointing that out before the words locked in my throat.

All the air escaped from my lungs and I wheezed out a startled swear word as the elevator doors slid closed, trapping me inside with him. I would have gladly shared the ride with a couple of brain-starved zombies instead of him.

Our eyes locked as all the animosity and hatred from two years ago radiated off him in waves.

"Justin," I squeaked out in a voice that was totally not my own.

"Selfish bitch," he greeted me with venom dripping from each word as he punched the button for the fifty-second floor with the side of his fist.

I cringed as the elevator walls began to close in on me. I knew he hated me. He had all but shouted it in my face the very last time we'd been in the same vicinity. His eyes and words had cut me like razorblades. Every syllable had traveled across the quad until all the students who had been lounging around had turned to stare at us with morbid fascination.

Justin was the love of my life.

Chapter Two

October 2010

I met Justin on a drizzly October day during my sophomore year at UW. I disliked him on sight. He was covered in equal amounts of tattoos and girls who giggled at every word that dripped from his lush lips. Everything about him screamed bad boy, from his ripped jeans and pierced eyebrow to his painted on white t-shirt. This combined with him smoking a cigarette pretty much sealed the deal for me. I'd lost my grandma to lung cancer a year ago. Ironically, she'd never smoked a day in her life, but my grandpa had smoked like a chimney before he passed away when I was five. Turns out all that crap they say about secondhand smoke isn't some mystical fairytale. That shit really does kill.

I ignored Justin and his admirers as I ordered a strawberry Danish and a coffee before setting myself up at a table under a large umbrella. I had a paper due the next day in my Teaching in Diverse Populations class. Usually, I preferred the café here to the library because it was closer to the dorms. Besides, my dorm room that morning had proved to be more of a distraction than an actual study haven. My roommate, Melissa, was a total sweetheart, but her constant interruptions made getting anything written nearly impossible. She was buzzing about some big Halloween party at Alpha Delta Phi the following week, and freaking out about what kind of costume she should wear as she frantically searched the Web for something original that would catch the eye of some guy. I told her to go as a Victoria's Secret Angel and she'd be all set. "You know, sexy panties and bra—add in a pair of wings and you'll have all the attention you want."

"I don't want to attract that kind of attention," she wailed, glaring at me.

"Hey, you said you wanted to snag a hunk. Your words, not mine," I pointed out dryly as I closed my MacBook. I lifted my backpack from the floor and stowed away my laptop and books.

"What about this one?" she asked, whipping her computer around to reveal a person covered in purple balloons.

"You want to go as an atom?" I asked, slinging my backpack over my shoulder.

"They're grapes, not an atom, smart ass."

"So wear the bra and panties underneath and then you can pop the balloons at an opportune time."

"Shut it," she snorted, throwing a pillow at me. "Wait, where are you going?" she asked as I headed for the door.

"Look, I love you despite the fact that you're a total spaz, but seriously, you make studying damn near impossible," I answered, throwing her a kiss.

"Do you want me to order you purple balloons?" I heard her call through the door as I headed down the hall.

I shook my head. She was a mess, but surprisingly, we'd really hit it off after a few initial speed bumps last year. I wasn't used to being around someone quite as vibrant and enthusiastic about everything as Melissa. Every emotion she was feeling was always on display for the world to see, like she was throwing up the Bat Signal or something. Everything was a big deal whether it was good or bad.

I was the polar opposite, not wanting the whole world to know every little detail about me. On our first night as roommates, I'd watched her with morbid fascination as she had buzzed around our room chattering nonstop about the great year we were going to have, and how we would be the best of friends. After hours of endless chatter, she had finally fallen asleep in the middle of regaling me with stories of all the parties and hot guys we would be exposed to now that we were in college. While she snored loudly in the bed next to mine, I vowed that first thing in the morning, I would do everything in my power to switch roommates, but by the time the next morning had dawned bright and early, she didn't seem nearly as bad. Of course, that was probably because she woke me with a steaming cup of coffee from the small kiosk near our dorm. Anyone that recognized the importance of a morning hit of caffeine couldn't be all that bad. I won't lie though; during the next few weeks I did question the sanity of that decision. Now, a year later, I was glad I didn't follow through with my initial plan. Sure, there were still times she wore on me, but she was pretty terrific all the other times. Even if she did act like a hyped-up RedBull junkie most of the time.

Leaving Melissa to her costume dilemma wasn't that much of a hardship. Despite the dreary day, I enjoyed sitting by myself at one of the cafés just off campus. I was supposed to be doing my schoolwork, but people watching kept distracting me while I sipped my coffee and nibbled on a sinfully good Danish that practically melted in my mouth.

I was halfway through my second cup of coffee and finally working on my paper when the annoying squeals from a nearby table broke my concentration.

"What about this one?" a girl asked in one of those fake baby-talk kinds of voices that got on my nerves. I could practically hear her eyelashes batting.

"Well, sweetheart, I designed that one when I was seventeen. The other half is here," a masculine voice drawled behind me.

"Oh my god. On your thigh? I want to see," another voice squealed so loud that I'm sure dogs halfway across the state were sent into a barking frenzy.

"I'm not that easy, babe," the same masculine voice chuckled as he answered. "What are you willing to trade?"

"Oh brother," I said louder than I intended. The sudden silence behind me clued me in that my comment had been heard. Now was one of those times I wished my best friend Tressa was here. She hated when girls made an ass of themselves by fawning over some guy. Better her making the loudmouth comment than me.

"You mean, like, I'll show you mine, if you show me yours?" the same piercing voice asked after a few awkward moments had passed.

I waited to hear what his response would be, completely annoyed with myself for paying attention to their conversation. I fought the urge to turn and look at Mr. Sure of Himself to see what had the two girls so entranced.

"You have no interest in seeing my art?" he asked into my ear, making me jump.

I silently berated myself for jumping. "Excuse me?" I asked, taking in his rugged appearance. He had nice eyes, I'd give him that, but the typical bad boy getup made any interest I may have had go down several notches. It seemed like he was trying too hard to portray his image. Even the drenched white t-shirt that showed his six-pack abs and a well-defined chest covered in tattoos was a complete turnoff. I wondered what he would have done had it not been raining.

Suddenly, I found myself laughing at a mental picture of him using a garden hose to soak himself down.

"What's so funny?" he asked, seeing that I was trying not to laugh. Without waiting for my answer, he pulled out an empty chair. The heavy metal squawked loudly across the concrete as he scooted himself toward the table.

"Why don't you sit down," I said sarcastically. "And get rid of the cigarette," I added, not caring that I didn't even know him.

His lips quirked at my testy tone before looking down at the cigarette. I expected him to scoff at my demand or even ignore it, but he surprised me by using the sole of his shoe to put it out. He earned a few more brownie points by placing the butt in his pocket versus throwing it on the ground.

"Won't your 'girlfriends' wither away into a pile of simpering drama now that you've left them?" I asked, casting a look over my shoulder where the two blonde bombshells were staring daggers into my back.

"Nah, they're cool," he said, flashing them a smile, which must have been laced with some kind of potion considering the way they both smiled back at him with such adoration. I was disgusted. He was nothing but a flirt who treated women with little respect.

"I think I'm going to hurl," I commented, making him turn his attention back to me.

He laughed. "You're hardcore. So, I'm getting the sense you don't like me. Is it because I interrupted your studying, or have we maybe hooked up before? Because I definitely think I would have remembered that."

"Please, I shudder at the thought. Does that crap actually work?" I sniped. The fact that he was callous enough to find nothing wrong with flirting with me while he was on some weird ménage-a-trois date was irritating as hell.

My comment only spurred more laughter from him. "I think you just broke my heart," he said, clutching his chest.

"I'm sure your playboy bunnies will be more than willing to repair it."

"How about you make it up to me by going out with me?"

This time it was my turn to laugh. "Um, no thank you."

"Why not?" he asked with genuine curiosity.

"Because, I don't like you," I answered, stating the obvious.

"How do you know? You don't even know me."

"Maybe not directly, but I know your type."

"My type?" he asked, ignoring the calls he was getting from the girls at the other table.

"Okay, let's forget for a moment how you're over here flirting with me while your fan club over there is cooling their heels waiting for you. I'm a little puzzled what they see in you, but the fact that they're dumb enough to actually share you makes me believe you must be an out-of-work musician or something like that. Guitar player, right?"

He threw his head back, laughing loudly at my analysis. "Wrong on both. I couldn't play an instrument to save my life. Not to mention, I'm pretty much tone-deaf. As for your first assumption, neither of them is my girlfriend. I met them at a party last night and agreed to meet up for coffee today. But enough about them. I'm curious to know why you came up with these assumptions?" he asked, sitting back in his chair and folding his arms across his chest while he casually crossed his ankles.

"Hmm, could it be the Barbie twins you're stringing along? You may not think you're dating them, but they sure think something is going on," I said, deliberately cutting my eyes in their direction. "Or, it could be all the ink. Is it a fetish, or are you just blatantly seeking attention? Your whole persona screams 'misunderstood tortured soul.' I'm guessing your parents ignored you and this is a vain attempt to get their attention," I added with complete disinterest. A hint of what almost looked like disappointment flashed in his eyes, but was gone in a second, convincing me I was imagining things.

"Are you one of those fortune tellers?" he drawled. "Hey, what number am I thinking of? Kidding. What about you? Gotta be a psych major, right?" he asked, raising his pierced eyebrow, which I failed miserably at ignoring.

"Education," I answered, holding up my Teaching in Diverse Populations book.

"And you moonlight as some kind of psycho-analyzer? Watching and judging everyone?" he asked.

I bristled at his description. I wasn't some busybody who clucked her tongue judgmentally anytime someone did something I disagreed with. That was my mom's thing. Not mine. Okay, so I liked to watch people, but that was different. It's not like I ever said anything negative, at least out loud. God, was he right? Did occasionally thinking snarky thoughts while nosing into people's business make me no different than my mom? It had to be different. Besides, who didn't do that? Was there a sane person who could actually walk through Walmart without judging someone? I pondered these questions as Mr. Wet T-shirt continued to eye me.

"I'm just observant," I finally answered lamely. "So, if you're not some misunderstood musician, what are you?"

"Like, what species? Well, when I was younger I pretty much assumed I was a monkey, but as I got a little older I was convinced either my parents were from another planet or I was. Recently, it's come to my attention that I might also be part ass," he answered cheekily.

"Funny," I answered, sitting back in my chair.

"I'll have to tell you what I am the next time I see you," he answered, standing up as his blonde companions called his name again in unison. "By the way, I'm Justin," he said, holding out his hand.

I held up my own hand, reluctantly. "It's been interesting."

"What, you're not even going to give me your name?"

"It's not like we'll be seeing each other again," I answered, knowing I sounded like a total bitch. I didn't see any point in encouraging something that was never going to happen.

"You never know. Maybe next time."

"That all depends on how many girls are in your entourage. If there is a next time, which I highly doubt," I pointed out, tugging at my hand that was still clasped in his.

"Well, until then," he said, giving my hand one last squeeze before releasing it. He strolled away from the table, not bothering to look back.

I could hear Barbie One and Two pouting about his absence as they headed in the opposite direction from where I was sitting. I didn't turn around, even though, for some insane reason I wanted to. I knew I'd never see him again, and most likely he'd forget about me before he even got to the next block. I may have come off as a total hag, but it was smart to not give in to the charms of some playboy. No matter how handsome he was. Yep, I definitely dodged a bullet.

About Author Tiffany

USA Today Bestselling author Tiffany King is a lifelong reading fanatic who is now living her dream as a writer, weaving Young Adult and New Adult romance tales for others to enjoy. She has a loving husband and two wonderful kids. (Five, if you count her three spoiled cats). Her addictions include: Her iphone and ipad, chocolate, Diet Coke, chocolate, Harry Potter, chocolate, zombies and her favorite TV shows. Want to know what they are? Just ask.

Web-authortiffanyjking.blogspot.com
Twitter-@AuthorTiffany
Facebook-Author Tiffany King

Other Woodfalls Girls Novels

No Attachments
A Woodfalls Girls Novel

USA Today Bestseller, available now as an ebook. Paperback available October 2014 from the Berkley Publishing Group. Published by the Penguin Group (USA) Inc.

Ashton Garrison walked away from her current life to escape the one thing she is unwilling to face. She knows her decision may be selfish, but in the end, leaving will be far less painful for everyone. She now has one goal: live life to the fullest with no regrets and no attachments. What Ashton doesn't count on is how fate always seems to find a way to screw up any good plan. Nathan Lockton specializes in locating a mark. He's done it over and over again--no attachments and no emotion necessary. What he thought was a routine lost and found job has forced Nathan to deal with something he has always ignored--his feelings. He's never fallen for a target, and yet, he's never met anyone like Ashton. Now deep in a dilemma, Nathan must decide to follow his heart or complete the job he was hired to do.

Love can come when you least expect it. The question is: if the odds are stacked against you, how far are you willing to go for the one you love?

Cross Country Christmas is proud to be part of The Twelve NA's of Christmas.
12 New Adult Novellas. 12 Best Selling Authors.
November 2013.

Made in the USA
Middletown, DE
15 May 2019